MEASURED FOR MURDER

MEASURED
FOR
MURDER

A FORSYTH AND HAY MYSTERY

JANET BRONS

TOUCHWOOD
EDITIONS

Edited by Frances Thorsen
Designed by Pete Kohut
Proofread by Claire Philipson
Cover image: *Tower of London* by Lawrence Sawyer, istockphoto.com
Author photo by Emma Leonhardt

LIBRARY AND ARCHIVES CANADA CATALOGUING IN PUBLICATION
Brons, Janet, 1954–, author
Measured for murder / Janet Brons.
(A Forsyth and Hay mystery)

Issued in print and electronic formats.
ISBN 978-1-77151-222-0 (softcover)

I. Title. II. Series: Brons, Janet, 1954–. Forsyth and Hay mystery.

PS8603.R653M43 2017   C813'.6   C2017-900368-2

We acknowledge the financial support of the Government of Canada through the Canada
Book Fund and the Canada Council for the Arts, and of the province of British Columbia
through the British Columbia Arts Council and the Book Publishing Tax Credit.

The interior pages of this book have been printed on 100% post-consumer
recycled paper, processed chlorine free, and printed with vegetable-based inks.

PRINTED IN CANADA AT FRIESENS

21 20 19 18 17   5 4 3 2 1

To Ian, who always expects the best from me,
and gives that of himself

PROLOGUE
England
February 1998

Susan Beck of Penicuik, Scotland, joined the rowdy group at the bar next door to the Wilkommen hostel. It was about six, and she was hungry. Her companions were an interesting mixture of Americans, Germans, Australians, and French. They were all roughly the same age, and split pretty evenly along gender lines. Some had been staying at the hostel for a couple of months; some, like Susan, had only been there a week or two. Apparently, years ago, a tradition had been established that the residents of the hostel would meet up around six for a drink and a bite to eat. The tradition had somehow stuck despite the hundreds of changes in clientele.

The next-door bar was old but not historic, run-down but not charming, dim but lacking in ambience. It was, however, clean and inexpensive, and while the food was pedestrian, it was filling. So the Drop Inn did quite a good trade from the young tourists from the hostel. The young people didn't cause a lot of trouble, apart from the odd problem due to an excess of drink and testosterone. Nothing untowards had happened lately, though. The worst the staff had had to put up with was the noise and laughter of the travellers as they recounted their latest adventures.

Susan felt comfortable here. Everyone was friendly and happy, and seemed to welcome her as an old friend. The banks in the booths were wide and comfortable, and she didn't have to squeeze onto some skinny wooden chair. Susan kept to herself, always a bit shy in company, but she enjoyed watching the others and hearing their stories.

She ordered a Coke and spaghetti bolognese. She looked at a few posters on the wall that she hadn't noticed before—mostly ads for long-forgotten concerts or advertisements for money-lending operations.

"Mind if I join you?"

Susan started, then looked up into the face of the young man who'd helped her get back to the hostel the other day.

"Of course," she said, then faltered, "I mean, no, I don't mind at all."

He ordered a pint and asked Susan how her visit was

going so far. She told him what she had done in the last few days, including a coach trip to Hampton Court. As she looked at him in the dim light, she realized he wasn't as unattractive as she had thought at first.

At his home in Pimlico, Detective Chief Inspector Hay was looking into the cost of hotels in Paris during early February. This was a pleasant enough task, although he was beginning to realize that he and Forsyth had left much unsaid during their telephone conversation, and that he had a number of decisions to make. *One room or two? Two, definitely two. Mustn't be presumptuous.*

He took a swig of coffee and listened to the rain sluicing down outside. Would they each be paying for their own room? Yes, no doubt Forsyth would insist. What sort of price range? This was tricky. He didn't want them to go to a dump, but prices were high in Paris, even in February, and he had no idea what her financial situation was.

He lit a cigarette and took a long drag. What part of Paris? No idea. For how long? She had said "a few days," but he wasn't sure exactly what that meant. In fact, they had decided virtually nothing during their phone call the previous day.

Hay decided to propose a series of options. Scenarios, hypotheses, the sort of thing the police were expected to come up with. Three hotels, ranging in price and location. Must also check out what was going on at museums and theatres and such. Or did she go in for that sort of thing? Hay was beginning to realize that he didn't really know much about Liz Forsyth at all. Not a clue, really. But he did want to find out. He could come up with a few more scenarios concerning things she might want to do.

He took another drag from his cigarette, reviewing the notes he had been scribbling about the trip. Suddenly the phone rang, interrupting his pleasant, if somewhat confused, thoughts about the proposed holiday.

Superintendent Neilson sounded tense, and his voice was about an octave higher than usual.

"We have another one," he said. "Young woman, long hair, naked, large. In a small park in Battersea. I want you there immediately."

Hay took down the details and hung up the phone. He squashed out his cigarette and mechanically put on his raincoat and boots. *Another one*, he thought. *Surely not.* But it sounded sickeningly similar. He locked the door behind him. This was not going to be a good day. Another murder—maybe one of Wilkins's "cereal killers?" He realized unhappily that he wouldn't be able to go away any time soon. *And now*, he thought, *I'll have to tell Forsyth.*

ONE

England
February 1998

Detective Chief Inspector Hay returned from the murder scene in a foul mood. Despite the crime scene tape and perimeter of uniformed officers, one particularly nosey journalist managed to buttonhole him on the way back to his Rover. Hay had never seen him before.

"I'm sorry," Hay said stiffly, "but there's nothing I can tell you at present."

The angular young reporter, trotting along beside the

taller man, continued. "It's much like the other killing, though, isn't it? Naked, heavy woman?"

That was true enough. He was not, however, about to discuss any of that with some oily journalist, not even to ask him how he knew so much. Hay had been deeply affected by the sight of the victim: her young body exposed, pale skin almost translucent, startling in the dull February light. Her skin was unblemished, except for the mark. That strange mark on her right hip. She looked as though she had simply fallen asleep.

"Nothing I can say right now," said Hay, relieved to reach the squad car. Detective Sergeant Wilkins, already in the driver's seat, had anticipated his boss's irritation and floored the gas the instant Hay slammed the door. The reporter gazed after the departing car, then slowly put his pen and small notepad back into his coat pocket.

His scruffy-looking photographer trailed up to him, professional-grade camera slung around his neck, hair blowing across his face. Without a word, they walked briskly together in the direction of their car.

Canada

"Well," said Liz, affecting her best Bogart impression—which wasn't very good—"we'll always have Paris."

"We'll never bloody have Paris at this rate," grumbled Hay, slumped over his desk, phone in hand. He had called her long-distance from his office in London. He would never have taken such a liberty with the office phone under usual circumstances, but was feeling uncommonly insubordinate at the moment.

Liz was at home prior to leaving for work in Ottawa. Hay's early-morning phone call had come as a surprise, especially as they had spoken only the previous day, clumsily planning a short vacation in Paris—the first time they were to meet since their joint investigation at the Canadian High Commission in London.

"When I nick this guy," Hay muttered, "he'll have more than a prison sentence to worry about."

Liz smiled despite her disappointment over their doomed holiday plans. She was sitting in her kitchen in Aylmer, Quebec, gazing blankly at her dog, vaguely wagging his tail by the door.

"So," she said, "this murder was similar to the first?"

"Virtually identical, so far as I can see. Waiting on forensics of course but hard not to draw a parallel between the two. White, naked, large women. Apparently smothered to death and left with an illegible mark on the right hip."

Liz knew that the first corpse, discovered only weeks ago, had been that of a young woman from Montreal, Sophie Bouchard.

"Do you know where she's from?" she asked, hoping this wouldn't be another Canadian innocent.

"No," he said shortly, butting out his cigarette. "Oh," he said, realizing what she meant. "I'll let you know as soon as possible. No reason to suspect it's another Canadian though."

"Well," said Liz, as breezily as she could manage under the circumstances, "clearly you'll be grounded for a while until this maniac is caught. Can't be helped."

"No," he agreed, "can't be helped. But I was really looking

7

forward to seeing you again," he said, in some combination of anger and despondency.

"Me too," said Liz. Her dog, Rochester, had begun to whine. He'd been sitting patiently by the door for some fifteen minutes and needed to go out.

"I'd best get on with it, then," said Hay grimly.

"Yes, of course. Talk soon?"

Hay grunted his assent and they hung up.

Liz walked dully to her garage, then struggled to pull open its wooden double doors, their bottom edges wedged into overnight snow. She grabbed a nearby shovel and dug, hurling the snow aside in mounting frustration, upset more than ever that their plans for Paris had been derailed. Rochester watched her intently from the porch, aware that her mood had changed for some reason.

When she had cleared enough snow to get the car out of the garage, Rochester jumped onto his towel on the back seat and Liz drove to her elderly neighbours' house to drop him off for the day. She exchanged pleasantries with Rochester's second family, the Greens, who were always pleased to see the shaggy, black dog. Rochester growled playfully at his old friend Monique, the Greens' elderly poodle, and they bounded off together into the living room.

Liz got back into her frosty Honda and began the drive into Ottawa. Light, powdery snow was blowing sideways across the windshield and the traffic was, as always, bumper to bumper. It was like this every winter morning as commuters waited to get onto the Champlain Bridge, which was one of the few crossings from the Quebec side of the river to Ottawa. White exhaust fumes poured from the cars lined up in front of her. Some people hadn't bothered to defrost their windows and struggled to peer outside while the frost melted. Those without a garage began their commutes with tall piles of snow, like oversized ice-cream cakes, sitting on their car roofs. The snow, in dirty, icy tracks in front of her car, looked especially grimy this morning, and the traffic was more than usually slow. Snowbanks glistened along the sides of Aylmer Road.

Liz was irritated and short-tempered, and realized how much she had been looking forward to a holiday with Hay. She was briefly annoyed with him, although she knew full well he wasn't to blame because a serial killer had invaded his patch. She huddled more deeply into her standard-issue overcoat, waiting her turn to cross the bridge, to warm up, to get to work.

TWO

England

The work of the Canadian High Commission in London continued apace, despite the absence of a High Commissioner. In the view of many of the staff, not having one had actually been an improvement. It could be difficult to work under political appointees; such people often had their own agendas and ambitions, which only occasionally coincided with those of the Canadian foreign policy establishment. The Acting Head of Post, Paul Rochon, was a reasonable, seasoned professional, and the High Commission had been conducting its affairs in a relatively relaxed, confident manner since the departure of Wesley Carruthers. This brief respite was almost over, however, as Ottawa had finally chosen a replacement High Commissioner.

Paul Rochon stepped into the stylishly furnished office of the Programme Head for Cultural Affairs, Sarah Farell. Sarah had scored one of the better offices in the High Commission and decorated it in a manner she thought befitted her position.

Rochon had dropped in to meet a young Canadian artist perched nervously on the edge of an armchair. "Congratulations," said Paul. "I believe it's very difficult to get these Canada Council grants."

"I'll say," said the young man enthusiastically. He was having some trouble controlling his excitement. "To be honest, I don't know anybody else who has ever got one." He picked up his coffee cup nervously.

Sarah smiled at both men from behind her desk and nodded. "Your work must be very impressive," she said to the artist.

The young man reddened and mumbled, "I hope so. It's an honour."

Rochon was genuinely pleased for the young man, Simon Simms, whom he understood to be a promising painter who had received a grant to stage a small exhibit in London. Paul's mind was, however, on other things at the moment. The new High Commissioner would be arriving the next day, and Paul was dreading it.

"So what's your plan?" asked Paul, trying to refocus on the eager young painter.

"I'm going to have an exhibit later this month, at a gallery in Pimlico—nothing terribly grand of course, but it's very exciting. I have some local contacts who will invite some guests, but I wonder if the High Commission might be able to help? Maybe some other, er, cultural contacts?" he asked, blushing more deeply than before. "And, of course, if there was any chance of a bit of money for drinks or whatever at the exhibit . . ." Simms trailed off and studied his shoes.

"I'm sure that Ms. Farell can tell you what support the High Commission might be able to provide," said Paul agreeably, glancing at his watch. "I'm very sorry, Simon, but I must go now. I'm in the midst of arrangements for the arrival of our new High Commissioner tomorrow morning."

If Simms hadn't been so excited by his luck, he might have noticed that Rochon pronounced this in a somewhat strangled tone. His Programme Head did notice, however, and tried to flash Paul a smile of encouragement.

"I'll leave you two to sort of out the details, then. Congratulations again," Paul added absently, leaving the office deep in thought.

DCI Hay had dispatched a team—consisting of Wilkins and Police Constable Etheridge, plus a new detective constable, Andrew Bell—back to the Wilkommen in case the second victim had also bunked there. Pictures of the young victim were produced for identification purposes.

The caretaker of the Wilkommen, Neil Connor, recognized the picture of the young woman, and said that he thought her name was Susan but had never spoken to her. But yes, she had been staying at the hostel. Connor pointed to a backpack he thought belonged to the girl. DC Bell, gloved, picked it up gingerly for transfer to forensics.

Connor appeared upset, perspiring heavily under the yellow-brown smock that was his janitorial uniform. DS Richard Wilkins noted that it took the caretaker some time to hand the photo back to the officers. Breathing noisily, Connor asked no one in particular who could have done such a thing.

Wilkins reassured the caretaker that the police were doing everything in their power to track down the killer, and asked Connor his whereabouts during the period the murder occurred. Connor, startled, blurted out that he had been "at 'ome, I work afternoons and evenings, see, and I would have been at 'ome." He was divorced, lived alone, and couldn't confirm his story. Nor could he recall anything else about the victim or her movements. Wilkins handed him a card anyway, asking him to call if he remembered anything later on. Connor put Wilkins's card into one of his deep pockets, where it joined several crumpled tissues, a couple of pound coins, and a set of keys.

No one at the hostel or the Drop Inn, the licensed establishment next door, had been able to provide the identity of the dead girl to the police, nor did anyone seem to know much about her. Two youths agreed her name might have been Susan but had no further information. Not that young people frequenting a place as casual and transient as a hostel were about to note surnames or addresses anyway.

Hay was reviewing crime scene reports. It was growing dark and he occasionally took a sip of stale black coffee in an effort to stay sharp. The second murder of a young woman was as mysterious as the first. Worse, in that they didn't even have an ID this time.

He went back to the earliest reports. According to the forensic pathologist, the murder had taken place between about 9:00 PM and 4:00 AM on February 7 or 8. The victim had been spotted by an elderly man walking his spaniel alongside the fencing on a narrow pathway leading to a scruffy grove of trees. The man, whose joints had seen better days, stumbled home as quickly as he could and called the police. He gave his name and address and, his voice shaking violently, assured police that neither he nor his dog had in any way interfered with the crime scene.

The girl's body lay in the corner of a large parking lot backing on to a crumbling block of flats slated for demolition. The property was surrounded by bright blue steel fencing, but it had failed in places and been vandalized in others. It probably hadn't been too difficult to break into, but why would a young girl end up there? Drugs? Sex? Booze? Surely there were more agreeable surroundings than that for a party. The body, Hay thought (he hated the word "corpse" and consciously tried to avoid using it), was eerily reminiscent of that of Sophie Bouchard, the murdered tourist from Montreal.

He looked again at the thick file of photographs from the crime scene. This girl was also lying on her side, glossy dark hair draped over her cheek, eyes closed, no evident trauma.

Heavy, naked, no jewellery. As in Sophie's case, the muddy ground around the body was disturbed and smeared. No immediate evidence of sexual assault. Hay wasn't a betting man, but if he were, he would have staked a tidy sum on there being alcohol and the date-rape drug Rohypnol in her system. He would have to wait on microscopic testing for definitive word on her blood results, and for conclusive evidence that no rape had taken place. But this crime looked more than familiar.

This scene was only about a mile from that of the first murder. Sophie Bouchard's body had been found behind a council estate, Hay recalled, on January 5. Just over a month ago. Sophie had been staying at a nearby hostel, the Wilkommen.

Some photos of the dead girl were strewn across Hay's desk and he studied them closely. He looked with particular interest at the mark on her right hip, drawing the Bouchard photos from a folder and comparing the marks. They were similar, but not identical. Short words, beginning with an *F*. Or was it an *R*? It looked more like an *R* on the second body, but it was impossible to be sure. He'd withheld the information about the mark from the press, so the chances of this being a copycat murder were remote.

His phone rang.

"Hay."

"Sir, there's a reporter on the line, a Jake Lombardy, says he's from the *Sun*. He says he spoke to you at the crime scene and would like to follow up. He's, er, quite persistent, Sir," added the constable anxiously.

"Tell him no," said Hay shortly. "There's a press conference tomorrow morning at ten. There's nothing more I can tell him now."

Hay hung up, irritated. Probably that skinny fellow who had followed him to the car in the morning. He slumped back into his chair and stared out the window. It was raining now, and a gusty wind was occasionally blowing raindrops sideways across the glass. Hay slugged back the dregs of the coffee, wincing a bit at their staleness.

Hay was unhappy to have been reminded about the press conference—he hated the damn things. At least he wasn't the lead on this—Superintendent Neilson seemed to thrive in the spotlight—but he still had to work out which details could be presented to the press, draft talking points for his boss, and liaise with the press relations office.

"Nothing to do with solving the bloody crime," he muttered to himself, but got on with it.

THREE

A pale, blue-eyed man sat in an overstuffed chintz armchair, one of the few items of furniture in the flat. He had rented it "fully furnished," the furnishings consisting of a sagging sofa, a wooden table with two avocado acrylic dining chairs, two battered side tables, and the gaudy flowered armchair in which he was sitting. A small television, rarely watched, sat on a low table across from the sofa.

It was sick, of course—even he knew that. But necessary. Or at least inescapable. Taking a large gulp of his Heineken, he knew he should be extremely content. Things had gone extremely well of late. News coverage of the killings. Revenge. The satiation of the thirst, if only temporarily.

He surveyed the uncomfortable flat with mild eyes. Why had this become necessary? His mind stalled as though stuck in a skipping long-play record. He leaned back, closing his eyes against the bare surroundings. Yes, Emma, his poor sister. Lost her job, took her life.

He repeated this mantra to himself again: *lost her job, took her life*. Those few words provided him the only motivation he needed. *Lost her job*. Fired from her lucrative, prestigious modelling job just because she had gained a couple of pounds and despite the vomiting and the laxatives had been unable to lose them. She looked like a skeleton even then, wasted skin hanging from what had once been triceps, spine sticking out through a thin coating of skin—jarringly reptilian, collarbones like razor blades. "Death warmed up," his mother had said, when her daughter was alive. Mother. All the women in the family were full figured. Until Emma.

Bastards, he thought, rousing himself and taking another swig of lager. *Bastards. Bunch of gay bastards running the fashion industry. Thinking the only attractive woman was thin, androgynous, not remotely female.*

Emma had been the exception in his family, even the extended version. She was smart, ambitious, and extraordinarily beautiful. He couldn't figure out where her looks came from, as the rest of them ranged from ordinary to decidedly unattractive. But Emma was stunning. Wide-set dark eyes fringed with naturally long, thick black lashes. The cheekbones the fashion industry so craved. Gleaming, chestnut-coloured hair hanging straight down her back. Tall, slim—no, he reminded himself, not slim. Skeletal.

She had entered, and won, some local beauty pageants while a young teen, catching the attention of an international modelling agency along the way. Before long there had been contracts for magazines, catwalks, and television. Most models might do well at one or perhaps two of these parts of the job, but Emma excelled at all three. Soon she was jetting off to the fashion capitals, spending a lot of time in Paris and even New York, to the pride and delight of her lower middle-class family. He remembered the thrill of seeing her picture on magazines as he passed through the till at the supermarket. He was three years younger than her, and her career guaranteed him instant cool in his school. They had been very close.

There was a pair of identical twins as well—stubby, rambunctious boys rarely out of trouble—but Emma and her younger brother were special friends. They always spoke when she phoned home. In fact, he recalled with a painful combination of fondness and despair, it had been Emma who'd flown all the way back from New York to nurse him through his concussion and dislocated shoulder, results of a football injury. His mother, he remembered, had been too busy working to support the family, or getting drunk, to take much care of him. Well, no, not working: if he was honest she was just getting drunk.

Emma told him that the magazine and television gigs paid a lot of money, but it was the runway work she enjoyed most. She had told him that the preparations for a fashion show provided her a tremendous rush—"rush" was her word. He had wondered about that—he had heard about a lot of drug use among models. But he never asked her and she offered nothing.

Then, when she hit her late teens, for the first time she began battling her weight. Battling herself, he thought, because that's what she was doing. The family was big boned, the women ample. But Emma loved her work and began starving herself to stay thin. Vomiting after meals, taking laxatives by the handful. She started chain-smoking to keep her metabolism up and weight down. The meals that she did consume consisted largely of hard alcohol, which, the other models told her, didn't have real calories. She admitted all this in a phone call from Paris, telling him not to worry, that all the girls did it. She also told him that jockeys resorted to these measures, as they had to be weighed, carrying their saddles, prior to every race. He wondered absently why that particular fact had stayed with him.

Her self-destructive efforts worked for a while, but the side-effects of all this abuse soon began showing on her face. Even at her young age, her eyes were beginning to sink—deep orbs replaced the sparkling, lustrous eyes of only months before. Her cheeks hollowed, making her once lovely cheekbones appear to jut sharply from her face. She looked almost frightening.

And still the weight crept back. At 5 feet 9 inches tall, she was almost 120 pounds—virtually obese by modelling standards. Then came the fresh faces: the new "it" girls, the next "Face of 1996," the new crop of fourteen-year-olds advertising anti-ageing cream on television. The thin, sexless children pouting their way down the catwalk.

The contracts dried up almost overnight. Emma's brilliant career was over.

He had looked forward to her returning home, to them spending time together like they had in the old days, before the fame and the money, the glitz and the glamour. He'd imagined them going for a coffee to talk of this and that, or hanging out and showing off his famous sister to his friends. Maybe they would go to a film. She liked romantic comedies.

Of course that hadn't happened. *Took her life.* It was a combination of alcohol and pills, and might have been an accidental overdose. It wasn't. She had left a note. For him.

He could do nothing for her now. But he could try to right the wrong. He was doing his very best. He emptied the bottle of lager. They had to see the beauty in actual women, not the air-brushed, artificial creations of the graphic artist. They had to.

It was deeply unpleasant. He had often watched "true crime" programmes on television and had learned that killers often found sexual gratification in their crimes. There was no sexual gratification in this, though. That would be akin to incest. Nothing could be further from sexual gratification than drugging a woman senseless and smothering her. He was deeply disgusted by the whole affair. But he knew it had to continue. It had to be said; it had to be noticed. For Emma.

FOUR
Ottawa

Liz entered her cramped office and kicked off her boots. She hadn't even had the chance to take her coat off when a constable tapped on her door and advised her that the Super wanted to see her. She was surprised but unconcerned: she liked and respected her Super and knew the feeling was mutual. Anyway, since the successful resolution of the Laila Daudova murder investigation, Liz had mostly been tidying up paperwork.

A couple of minutes later, having straightened her jacket and shaken some snow from her hair, she passed through the

Super's open door. As usual, he was reading something and waved her in while he finished. Liz sat down across from his desk.

He took off his reading glasses and looked, unsmiling, at Inspector Forsyth. Liz noted that he didn't seem his usual ebullient self. In fact, he appeared uncharacteristically nervous—sombre, even. "Coffee?"

"Sure," she said, realizing this would be a longish meeting if coffee were on offer. They both stood up and walked together to the coffee pot at the end of the corridor. The Super insisted on paying and dropped the required change into the coffee fund tin.

"You notice the price went up?"

"Yeah," she replied with a short laugh. "Everything's going up," she added, unable to come up with anything more original.

They continued to exchange pleasantries as they participated in this small ritual. They both took their coffee black, but the Super added three heaping teaspoons of sugar to his. Each took a couple of sips of the coffee so as not to spill it on the way back.

"Stale," commented the Super.

Liz agreed, adding that it must have been left over from the night shift. The Super nodded, and they returned to their previous positions in his office. Liz still had no idea what she was doing there, but the Super finally began to speak.

"Well, Liz, you've had a very busy and successful couple of months. Several extremely complicated homicides, both with international repercussions. The Guévin murder at the High Commission and the killing of that furrier in London."

"Lester Wilmot."

"Yes, yes, poor Lester Wilmot," he said, his eyes unfocused as he watched the low, grey sky through his tiny office window.

"And then," he continued, gazing at Liz again, "the Chechen woman and her husband here in Ottawa. That took some damned good detection to get a result. All very well done."

Liz smiled her gratitude, but found it difficult to reconcile his words with his mood. He seemed anxious, almost skittish, and Liz kept her eyes on her boss as she took a sip of tarry coffee.

"You deserve a break," he said. "And so, I'd like to offer you a three-week training course at the Police Staff College at Bramshill, in Hampshire. Er, that's in England," he clarified, in response to the astonished look on his inspector's face. "They're doing some great training—cutting-edge forensics and the like—and they're opening up to international students. It could be very interesting for you, and useful to the Force. Starting in a week, though—you'd have to get your skates on."

Liz was stunned. Of course she would love to have a break, to go on a course, and to England, yet. She could even spend some time with Hay . . .

"There's one other thing I need to tell you, though. I'm being moved on. Not that far, as it happens, but interesting work. I'll be heading up the Criminal Investigation Policy Centre. It's a good assignment, and my wife is relieved that we're staying in Ottawa. She has some family here, so she'll be more than happy to stay here for a few more years."

"Congratulations, Sir." Her initial excitement faded on hearing this unexpected announcement. "We'll miss you an awful lot around here." She meant it. He was one of the best she had worked for. But she still couldn't make out why he seemed so tense, especially with a promotion in his future. She paused, then asked, "Do you know who will be replacing you?"

The Super looked at her intently. "I do. Superintendent Murray Purcell."

Liz flinched. She had never worked for Purcell but knew him well by reputation. And that reputation was decidedly disagreeable. To Liz's knowledge, Purcell was an oily character, well known for psychological harassment towards subordinates in general and women in particular. She had heard many stories of Purcell's vulgarity, sexual advances, and taste for revenge if and when he was rebuffed.

She also knew that most of these women hadn't reported him because of the potential damage to their own careers. It wasn't a good idea to blow the whistle on a superior, especially for sexual misconduct. It was more likely that the women themselves would be blamed, rather than the offender himself being called to book. Some complaints had gone up the chain over the years but were never heard about again. Usually the female complainant was simply moved on to another assignment. So Purcell got away with it—his brutish personality seemingly coated with Teflon.

"Purcell," she murmured, unaware of having said anything.

"Yes," said the Super.

Suddenly she asked, "Is that why you want me gone?"

He reddened. "I hoped you wouldn't take it the wrong way. I had in fact been thinking that you deserved to be sent on a course even before I heard who was replacing me. You can have a cigarette if you want to."

Liz, surprised, gratefully accepted the offer as he opened the small window a crack. She reached into a pocket and pulled out one of several colourful Bics and a pack of cigarettes. Lighting one, she said, "So you're trying to protect me?"

"I know you're a big girl, Liz. But you're also a fine officer. You don't need to be stuck with a misogynistic jerk like Purcell." He went to his window and opened it a few inches. "A few weeks away and maybe you can think things over, apply for another assignment. It would give you a bit of breathing room."

"When's he coming in?"

"In about a week."

"So soon?" she asked, surprised.

He nodded. "I'm really sorry I couldn't say anything earlier, but both moves have just now been confirmed," he said with an involuntary glance at his telephone. "Had to keep my mouth shut. Anyway," he said dolefully, "gave me a chance to look into the course. Timing looked good to me."

Liz gave him a grateful smile and took a long drag from her cigarette. "How has he gotten away with it for so long anyway?"

Her boss shook his head in irritation. "Nothing's ever stuck. Nobody upstairs *wants* anything to stick. And don't forget his relatives."

Liz remembered that Purcell was from a moneyed, well-connected Toronto family, generous contributors to political finances.

"So it's easier to look the other way and just move the women around."

"A few of us have tried to get the powers that be to do something about him," he said, reddening again, "but nothing is ever done."

Liz nodded.

"So what do you think about the training course?"

Liz realized that he'd been anxious she might be annoyed that he was trying to keep her out of Purcell's line of fire. He needn't have worried. The choice between a well-deserved break for training, in England of all places, or fighting off the advances of a smutty superior was pretty clear. She stubbed out her smoke and smiled broadly. "I think it sounds like a great idea. For lots of reasons." She smiled. "Ottawa in February, for instance. Thank you very much." The main reason, though, she kept to herself.

"So, buddy, it goes like this," said Liz, looking deeply into Rochester's bright, interested eyes. "I have to go away for a while."

Rochester whined softly. Not that he knew what Liz was saying, exactly, although he recognized her serious tone of voice, which made him miserable. He dropped his shaggy head, mutely asking for his ears to be scratched in consolation. Liz rubbed his ears and the top of his head, explaining, "You see, I'm being given a really great opportunity to go to England for a few weeks to train at the Police Staff Training College in Bramshill. You can't come with me, but I won't be long. Just about twenty big sleeps."

Rochester looked up glumly, then dropped his head back down for more scratches. He may not have understood everything, but he knew what he liked.

"Anyway, of course you'll go to Auntie Margaret and Uncle Bill's, and you can play with Monique as much as you like." Rochester recognized the word "Monique" and tentatively wagged his tail but didn't move his head.

After a couple more minutes of scratching and several more apologies to her dog, Liz got up from the floor and flopped onto her couch. Lighting a cigarette, she realized that she had not told Hay about her forthcoming visit. She looked at the clock and calculated the time difference, once again.

London

"There's a reporter here to see you, Sir," said the voice over the phone.

"Not that bloody Lombardy," said Hay, deeply annoyed. "Tell him that the information we have is all being shared with the press as we get it. I have nothing more to say."

"He says he has information."

"What?"

"Yes, Sir. Says he has some information about the killings of the young women and wants to talk to you personally."

"All right," said Hay doubtfully. He didn't expect the reporter would have much to say, but couldn't allow any potential lead to slip by. "Put him in Interview Two." He took a couple of last drags from his cigarette, crushed it out, and went to the interview room, carrying a cold mug of coffee.

Lombardy was already in the room, having been escorted in by PC Etheridge, who was now standing at the door. Lombardy had been sitting there for several minutes, staring at a white brick wall, feeling uneasy. He'd been in a room like this one a few times before, when he was scarcely out of his teens. *Stupid bitch*, he thought, *claiming it wasn't consensual. How was he to know she was too young? Dressed like a tart and looked like a hooker.* He had been lucky to get off with a warning, when the girl dropped charges. Laws had tightened up since then—he wouldn't make that mistake twice.

Lombardy looked around the room, disappointed. He'd hoped to be invited into the DCI's office, have a look around, see if he could spot some papers. Something. Anything. He needed to know how much the police knew. He tried to make some small talk with the haughty-looking officer by the door but was unsuccessful.

Hay entered the room with a gruff "Good morning," and took his seat. He took a good look at Lombardy for the first time. The reporter was dressed in a shiny brown suit with a striped yellow tie loosely knotted around his neck. He carried a dark overcoat of indifferent quality and wore a greasy fedora on his head. Hay thought Lombardy looked like a caricature of an American reporter from the 1940s, and half-expected to see a press card sticking out of his hat.

"I believe you have something to tell us, Mr. Lombardy." Hay made an effort to sound friendly.

"Any chance of a cup of tea?"

"No."

"Well, I'm just wondering if you think there might be another murder or do think he's done?"

"I thought you had something to tell us."

Lombardy laughed—a high-pitched, scratchy sort of laugh.

"More the other way 'round, really. Come on, Inspector," said Lombardy, settling himself in his chair and taking on a conspiratorial tone. "You must have more than your boss is saying at the press briefings. 'Course you do. There must be some similarities between the cases? Connections between the girls? An MO or something? I really could use a bit of information—nothing much, just something the others don't have. I'm pretty new here and could use a leg up on the story."

Hay was already on his feet. "No, Mr. Lombardy," he said. "I have nothing for you. You can leave now." He indicated the door, although Etheridge was already moving towards the reporter.

"But just something small, some detail none of the others have . . ."

"I've asked you to leave," said Hay with mounting irritation. "If you don't, I'll be happy to ensure that you do."

Etheridge had moved closer. "And you are, in fact, wasting police time."

Lombardy left quickly, under his personal police escort.

Hay was irritated. He didn't think much of the press in general and his opinion had not been improved by this latest encounter. He stopped by the desk of the PC who had initially phoned him. Under no circumstances was Lombardy to be let anywhere near the investigation, or near Hay himself.

"No, Sir," said the PC, hands trembling as he placed his pen back on the table. "I'll make sure of it, Sir." Hay had already slammed his door.

Ottawa

From long habit, Liz arrived at the airport early. Sergeant Gilles Ouellette, who had driven her and her luggage directly from the office, was sorry to see her go. Interesting things seemed to happen when Liz was around; his work with her during the last couple of months had been some of the most exciting of his career.

"Well, I hope it's an interesting course anyway," said Ouellette, glumly realizing his gas tank was getting low.

"It should be," said Liz. "I'll give you a call next week and let you know how it's going. As long as you do the same?" she added, raising an eyebrow.

Ouellette groaned but agreed to do so. He knew that the current Superintendent was moving on to greener pastures and was being replaced by a nasty piece of work called Murray Purcell as early as next week.

As they pulled up to the revolving door leading into the departure lounge, Ouellette added, "Oh, and give my best to DCI Hay." Liz reddened slightly but nodded. "And Wilkins too, of course." DS Wilkins was Ouellette's opposite number in London, and the two had struck up an instant friendship during the Guévin investigation, cemented by a lengthy "tour" of historic London pubs.

"Yes, of course I will. I don't know how much time I'll have to visit London, though," she said in a failed attempt to appear uninterested. "Thanks for the lift, Gilles. Take care of yourself."

"And you, Sir," he said, and they both grinned at their old joke.

Having checked in and received assurances the plane was on time, she went into the newly renovated bookstore and bought a copy of the *Economist*, her preferred airplane read. After a last quick cigarette outside the terminal, she went to what passed for a restaurant, bought herself a glass of wine, and once again perused the outline of her training course at the Bramshill Police Staff College. The classes looked fascinating, if a lot to cover in three weeks.

This was a new course being offered to international students. It was very expensive, the Super (or ex-Super, she thought sadly) had said, and she was grateful for the opportunity to study in such prestigious surroundings. Liz assumed that the tuition fees would go towards the upkeep of the stunning Jacobean mansion that housed the college and looked up at her from the cover page of the curriculum. She was unsure what to expect by way of classmates.

"Developments in Trace Evidence Analysis/DNA" (four days), she read, followed by "Serial Killers—Case Studies" (four days). This was not a subject with which Liz had much familiarity. Perhaps, she thought, she might find something useful for Hay. He had pronounced himself delighted that she would be coming to England, despite his being consumed by his own apparent serial killer. "That's wonderful," he had said. "I'll try to get this bloody mess sorted out before you get here, but don't hold your breath."

"Gaining Public Confidence and Trust" (two days), then "The Evolving Role of Computers and Databases in Crime-Solving" (four days). She took a sip of slightly yeasty red wine. Liz was disappointed that Hay wouldn't be meeting her on arrival at Heathrow, but of course he was consumed by his case. In any event, Bramshill protocol dictated that she would be met by a representative of the college and transported to lodgings on site.

Two tones gonged through the airport's sound system, followed by an incomprehensible, echoing message, and Liz resumed scanning the curriculum as though she had never seen it before. Of course she had read it through in detail many times already. "Management Styles" (one day).

Liz took another sip and was relieved that the management styles segment was a short one—in recent years she and her fellow officers had been subjected to a multitude of personality profiles and management style questionnaires dreamt up by self-styled management consultants. She reckoned that by now she could probably teach the course herself.

Later, seated in Economy, Liz scanned the in-flight

magazine and looked at the dinner menu. *Interesting*, she thought. Choice of chicken or lasagna. Not that long ago the choices had been between beef and chicken. Although not that long ago she would have been in Business Class. Regulations had changed and now any flight less than ten hours had to be in Economy.

She glanced up at a scowling, middle-aged air hostess who did not return her smile. *Or*, she wondered, *is it "air hostess" now? Or "stewardess?" Oh—that was it—"flight attendant."* Whatever the woman's title was, she grimly thrust a set of headphones at Liz and told her curtly that they had run out of cushions.

Liz sighed and leaned back in her seat, on which the neck rest was uncomfortably high. At least she had been assigned a seat in the row next to the emergency exit, which afforded a little more legroom. This, combined with her own diminutive stature, allowed her to get reasonably comfortable. She opened her *Economist* and stuffed her novel—Trollope's *Warden*—into the pocket next to the air-sickness bag and her box of nicotine gum. Soon the engines began thrumming in earnest and, just as it seemed they were about to taxi the entire way to their destination, Air Canada flight 866 lifted off and headed for London.

Liz would have been surprised to know that, seated in Business Class, was the new High Commissioner to the United Kingdom, one Lucien Roy. Liz had interviewed his predecessor in December, in connection with the murder of the chief Canadian Trade Commissioner within the walls of the High Commission itself.

The new High Commissioner perused his Business Class menu greedily—there was a much greater choice than was available in Economy. His seat was very comfortable, even for his considerable girth. There were few other passengers in Business, which suited Roy just fine. He put on his airline slippers, plugged in the airline headset, and propped a pillow behind his head. He was happy to spread out in comfort for the remainder of the flight.

FIVE

The flight landed at Heathrow some twenty-two minutes behind schedule, and Lucien Roy was irritated. But then, Lucien Roy, newly appointed Canadian High Commissioner to the United Kingdom, was often irritated. Not that there had been anything wrong with the flight, but he was fatigued and had developed nasty gas pain in his gut. He was supposed to be picked up by some Paul Rochon, who would be his flunkey at the High Commission.

Despite Roy's innate pomposity and condescension, he was really quite excited—not that he would have admitted it. Being named High Commissioner to London was a perk and an honour, payback for his long years strategizing in party back rooms, raising funds from corporations and unions, and long nights schmoozing with the great and the tiresome. He deserved this. Lucien Roy wasn't entirely sure what the job of High Commissioner actually entailed, but he was sure he deserved it.

Paul Rochon waited at Arrivals at Heathrow, trying to tell himself that the arrival of the new High Commissioner would take some of the load off. Share a bit of the work. He sighed deeply, knowing this wasn't to be the case, that if anything his workload would increase, as he tried to keep the new Head of Post from putting his foot in his mouth, making up policy on the spot, and alienating carefully nurtured allies. He sighed again. He had two more years in London. This was meant to be his dream posting, but so far it had been a never-ending nightmare. The kind in which you try to get somewhere but keep encountering obstacles, all the while knowing the clock is ticking and you're nowhere near your ultimate goal.

The jet had landed, and Paul nodded to a bored-looking official from Heathrow protocol. The two men headed across the runway to greet the new Canadian High Commissioner.

Liz stood in the aisle, waiting to disembark. The aircraft had landed some time ago, but no one was moving as people stood in the aisle of the plane, buckling under carry-on luggage. Others stood at their seats, heads cocked to one side to avoid hitting their heads on the overhead consoles.

The passengers were, Liz noticed, considerably quieter than they had been when boarding. It had been a long flight, if uneventful, and the chirpiest of holidaymakers appeared worn and sweaty. Even the babies who had set up a mighty squall on lift-off now appeared drugged and world weary. Eventually they began to "deplane"—a word that Liz always found weird—walking in that peculiar side-to-side motion seen only in aircraft.

Of course Liz was exhausted. She had never been a good flier, and despite her excellent reading material, a tolerable meal (she had chosen chicken on principle), and a couple of glasses of wine, she felt as though she'd been hit by a bus.

Chef Luciano Alfredo Carillo would never have admitted that he disliked the new Canadian High Commissioner on sight. He would, however, have allowed that he hadn't warmed to the new boss immediately. Lucien Roy had been introduced to the domestic staff on his arrival from Heathrow, the formalities being conducted by Paul Rochon. Roy would meet the professional staff the following day, after sleeping off some jet lag.

Carillo eyed the new High Commissioner and wiped his hands on a tea towel to shake hands. Before him, shoulders hunched, was a squat, jowly man with fleshy features, a bald pate, and no discernible waistline. Roy seemed a troubling combination of arrogance and anxiety, which rattled the chef, but Carillo rapidly pasted on a welcoming smile and revealed every one of his gleaming teeth. Pleasantries were exchanged, and Carillo told him the kitchen would be on standby for anything the High Commissioner might wish to order.

Roy looked somewhat taken aback by this, nodded abruptly, and shuffled out of the room followed by a defeated-looking Paul Rochon.

Carillo absently wiped his hands again on his tea towel. What should he expect from this one, he wondered. Would Roy be one to host lavish receptions and elegant dinners? Or would he prefer staying home on the nights he could, watching television and eating pizza? He had understood from an earlier conversation with Rochon that Roy was married, but that his wife would remain in Canada for several weeks before joining her husband in the United Kingdom. The chef figured he might not have a clear idea of what to expect from the new High Commissioner until Madame arrived.

Propping himself up against a kitchen counter, Carillo surmised that Roy seemed to enjoy his food, and, given his florid complexion, perhaps especially enjoyed sugar and alcohol. Other than that, it was difficult to gauge what demands would be made on the kitchen under the new regime. Carillo concluded it would be prudent to send up some tea and chocolate-covered digestive biscuits and, later, offer something more substantial. He reached for the kettle and plugged it in.

Paul Rochon deposited the new High Commissioner in his living quarters, happy to flee the scene. He returned to his office, aware that other members of staff were watching him with interest. They were doubtless hoping that Paul would relay his first impressions of the new Head of Post.

Paul closed the door behind him, not knowing exactly what he would have wanted to tell the staff anyway.

He sat in his office chair and loosened his tie. He wondered how much the staff knew of Roy's background. Paul hadn't known a lot himself but had made a few phone calls to old colleagues at Headquarters when the appointment had first been announced. No evidence of any wrongdoing had ever been made public, or at least nothing had ever stuck, but there was just a whiff of something a bit fishy about Roy. Something about fundraising he'd done for the Quebec branch of his party some years ago, some speculation about unsavoury connections to the construction industry.

Rochon again wondered why the Prime Minister had chosen Roy for this plum assignment. He figured there was probably some interesting backstory there. He pulled a few classified telexes out of his in-basket, all of which required a fast turnaround, but he had trouble getting his mind off his new boss.

On a personal level Roy was, perhaps, not as objectionable as Paul had expected, although the man was probably suffering from jet lag, which may have dulled his storied temper. Roy hadn't said much as he was conveyed in the official vehicle to the Official Residence, which backed onto the Chancery, or working quarters, of the High Commission. Roy had watched the scenery go past his window in silence. After a couple of attempts at starting a conversation, Paul abandoned the effort and looked out his own window at the shops and buildings and parkland flashing past. If the driver and butler, Anthony Thistlethwaite, had formed any opinions of his own about the new boss, he wouldn't have dreamt of voicing them.

Not just apprehensive about the new boss, Paul was concerned about his own future. It was unusual to have a francophone as both head of mission and second-in-command, especially as this was, obviously, an Anglo country. Would he be given his marching orders soon? He sighed again, gazing out his window onto a colourful throng of pedestrians in Grosvenor Square, which had appeared from nowhere to enjoy an unexpected sunny break between rain showers.

Nothing for it but to work as usual and try to adapt to the transition as well as possible. He drafted a quick message for Ottawa to report the safe arrival of the new High Commissioner and then turned his attention to reconfirming the arrangements for the Presentation of Credentials at Buckingham Palace.

SIX

Liz was exhausted from her flight and the hour-and-a-half drive from Heathrow to Bramshill Police Staff College. Her first view of the stately mansion was a blurry one, as the house was obscured by a thick morning mist, and her eyes were in much the same condition. The young police constable who had driven her from the airport courteously left her at the front entrance.

The air smelled of rich earth and moss. An indefinable smell of something sweet and floral lingered in the background. Liz didn't have much time to ruminate on the sights and smells, however, as she was immediately met by a mid-ranking officer from Scotland Yard. He gave her a quick tour of the college, and she noted with appreciation that there was a large library, a gymnasium, and a pub.

Then he took her to her small but comfortable quarters. She had no fixed appointments or duties until the following morning, although there was an optional reception that evening. She was looking forward to going to sleep but tried to reach Hay first. He was out, doubtless working his cases, but she was pleased to hear his voice on the answering machine and to know that at least they were in the same time zone.

Andrew Bell, a fledgling detective constable working his first murder, was elated by his assignment to the legendary DCI Hay's squad. Even minor involvement in the investigation of a possible serial murderer was exhilarating, and the new boss's reputation was first rate—particularly if one could ignore the odd complaint about Hay's uncompromising standards and short fuse.

Bell, now single, childless, and living alone in a small flat, was intent on making a good job of it. He was happy to work all the hours he could find to do his job and make a good impression. He had been attached to DS Richard Wilkins and a uniformed officer, PC Etheridge. DC Bell tried to make himself useful and willingly immersed himself in the many interviews that followed the second murder. Not yet seasoned enough to ask too many questions, he compensated by taking copious notes.

He watched DS Wilkins carefully, immediately recognizing that he was a skilled interviewer. Wilkins was always meticulously prepared; he knew exactly the type of information he needed but allowed the witness to explain, without interruption, what he or she had seen, heard, or thought. Bell recognized some of the techniques he'd learned during training: separating witnesses so they couldn't influence one another; minimizing distractions; asking open-ended questions. Wilkins somehow managed to come across as both sympathetic and authoritative in his dealings with potential witnesses. His tactful encouragement seemed to elicit information with apparent ease.

Wilkins's sidekick, though, PC Etheridge, struck Bell as haughty, fatuous, and capable of getting peoples' backs up without saying a word. Whether Etheridge was aware of it or not, he wore a perpetual sneer—not designed to inspire confidence in the general public.

Not that the general public seemed to have seen anything useful to the police. A string of shops located near the crime scene had, of course, been closed in the middle of the night and, while the local butcher lived above his meat shop, he had seen and heard nothing. Owners and staff of the second-hand clothing store, the corner grocery, the used booksellers, and the small Indian restaurant, Roti Chai, similarly had little to offer. A bakery had closed its doors long ago and was boarded up.

Residents of a nearby block of flats—a bleak, featureless structure—had been canvassed with little result. Much like the Sophie Bouchard case, the murder seemed to have been committed in a vacuum, with no sights or sounds to assist the police.

This, thought PC Etheridge with a sneer, *is a bloody bore.* He had known, of course, that police work wouldn't all be screaming sirens and car chases, but he had expected it to be a damn sight more interesting than this. Instead, here he was, traipsing from interview to interview, speaking with dull or uncooperative characters, and not a master criminal in sight.

At least, he thought, *someone is enjoying himself.* He was watching DC Bell, an earnest-looking, slope-shouldered young man who seemed to be having the time of his life. Evidently, he worshipped Wilkins.

While most of the members of the murder squad, both police officers and detectives, knew one another, at least by sight, a new, slightly intimidating character had been added into the mix as well. Inspector Gerrit de Jong was a visiting officer from the Dutch KLPD, the *Korps landelijke politiediensten*, or National Constabulary. De Jong was attached to the squad as the first officer in Britain under a recently introduced police exchange programme of the European Union.

De Jong was greeted with some suspicion within the confines of the incident room, despite his outgoing manner and impeccable English. Tall and broad shouldered, he had been introduced to the squad by DCI Hay during one of the morning briefings. In addition to his evidently not being a Brit and therefore being seen as something of an outsider,

De Jong had another shortcoming—one that was unforgiveable for the vast majority of squad members. He was almost intolerably handsome.

De Jong had the sort of healthy, slightly caramelized colouring that seems solely the province of the Dutch. Along with a head of thick blond hair, blue eyes, and an elegant stance, de Jong possessed an engaging manner and sparkling smile. As if this wasn't enough, he had clearly made inspector relatively early in his career, so he was not immediately welcomed by most, if any, of the male members of the murder squad. Whatever the female officers were thinking, they were at pains to appear unimpressed.

"Damn," muttered Hay through gritted teeth, having listened to Liz's message. He had missed her call, and now she was going to sleep. He didn't want to wake her by calling back.

He had just hung up the phone when it rang again. The backpack found at the hostel had been examined by forensics and the fingerprints had been sent for comparison. The contents were meagre: a toothbrush and tube of toothpaste, antiperspirant, a tube of hand cream, a bottle of two-in-one shampoo and conditioner, a hairbrush, a package of tampons nestled among several pairs of panties and socks, and two blouses—one pink and one patterned in black and red—in plus sizes. No identification or paperwork had been found.

The phone rang again. Hay sighed and picked up the receiver. It was Liz.

"I thought you were going to sleep," he said, trying not to sound as pleased as he felt by the sound of her voice.

"I tried," she said. "I'm absolutely bagged but couldn't nod off. Still have the sound of the engines in my ears." She paused, then added, "I hate jet lag."

He smiled in sympathy and asked how she liked her quarters.

"Nice," she said, "very nice actually. Cozy and private." She was listening to the rain patter against the window of her room, and gazing out at the acres of parkland surrounding Bramshill. She was comfortable—serene almost—in these surroundings. Part of her mind was wishing her parents had never decided to immigrate to Canada when she was a child. It was, she thought, a soft day.

"That's good," said Hay, unaware he had broken into such ruminations. "Have you met any of the other students yet?"

"No, they just gave me a quick tour and let me come in here to rest. There's supposed to be some kind of welcoming reception tonight, but honestly, I really would prefer to sleep."

"You should do then. You can meet the others tomorrow."

She mumbled assent.

"But," continued Hay, "try not to let the ghosts wake you up."

"Ghosts?" asked Liz, briefly alert. "What ghosts?"

"Oh, don't you know?" said Hay, smiling into the phone, "the place is haunted. Actually it's meant to be one of the most haunted houses in Europe. There are supposed to be some fourteen ghosts in the building."

"Really?" said Liz, genuinely interested. "I believe there's also a herd of white deer on the property somewhere."

"Yes, I've heard that too."

Clearly they were chatting about anything and nothing and might have done so indefinitely had Hay not finally asked, "So when do you think we can get together? Dinner someday soon, I hope?"

"That would be great," answered Liz. "I'll have to get a handle on the programme here and see what sort of spare time I have. I *think* the weekends are free, but you never know how many 'optional' mandatory things they plan on these courses. Anyway, I'll let you know as soon as I can and figure out how to get down to London."

"Wonderful," said Hay. "I don't know how I can get away from here with all this going on, although apparently there's a lovely little village called Eversley not far from you, which could be worth a visit." He looked at the reports covering his desk. "In an ideal world."

Liz nodded silently at the other end of the phone. All at once she felt utterly exhausted and wanted nothing more than to curl up under the duvet on her room's single bed and sleep for hours.

"So we'll talk when you've had a chance to look at your schedule, yes?"

"Yes, Stephen, we'll do that, soon. I'm suddenly awfully tired."

"You go to bed then. And forget about that bloody reception."

"So, it's going to be like this, is it?" fumed Chef Luciano Alfredo Carillo, fiercely regarding the half-eaten steak that had been returned to him from the new High Commissioner, with the comment that it was "too bloody." At least the roast potatoes had been consumed, and he imagined that there were slightly fewer green beans on the plate than when it was sent up. The pudding, at least, had been consumed in its entirety.

Carillo squinted at the scrawled note that had been returned with the remnants of the meal. *What on God's green earth*, wondered the proud Italian, *was poutine?* He couldn't have known that years later this concoction would become a popular Canadian classic—as far as he was concerned, cheese curds and gravy on fries sounded abominable.

SEVEN

At first, Hay hadn't been sure if the weight of the murder victims was coincidental, or if it had contributed to making them targets in the first place. The two girls looked similar in other respects. Female, obviously. Young, with long dark hair. *No*, he thought, driving back from the office during another downpour, *this isn't a coincidence*. He glowered, thinking of the television detectives who maintained that "there are no such things as coincidences." Bollocks. Of course there were. Coincidences occurred in everyday life and they happened in police work. But this, he admitted, was probably not one of them. This murderer clearly had a "type."

Why, though, would someone want to murder innocent women—at least for the moment he was assuming they were innocent—simply because they were carrying a few extra pounds? Well, okay, perhaps more than a few, but was he looking for someone with a pathological hatred of heavy women?

He considered the possibility that the second killing could be a means of disguising the fact that the first victim, Sophie Bouchard, had been the actual target. Or, it could have been the other way around, with Sophie's murder obscuring the fact that the latest victim was the killer's intended prey. That meant that it was vital to get as much information as possible about both girls, but made it all the more frustrating that the police had been unable to identify the second victim.

In some ways, the second murder was good news. It probably meant the killer was still around. While the murderer of Sophie Bouchard could have fled, never to be seen again, a second victim clearly implied the killer was either local or at least still in the vicinity. Did he live around here? Or work nearby?

In addition, the second murder meant that resources would no longer be siphoned off, at least for the immediate future. He had already lost some staff to other investigations when the Bouchard murder stalled, but the second killing had pushed the investigation back up to the top of the priority list. He even had an additional officer by way of Dutch

Inspector Gerrit de Jong. Hay wasn't sure he approved of the amount of integration and cooperation currently underway among the various European police agencies, but he wasn't about to complain about an extra pair of hands.

The murder squad was busy interviewing anyone who might have witnessed the second killing, including residents of a nearby block of flats, (which, in DS Wilkins's opinion, should have been condemned along with the one next to the crime scene). They were also canvassing the proprietors of a string of modest shops in the vicinity, but nothing particularly striking had emerged. Some CCTV cameras from the shops had been recovered and their recordings were being reviewed, but so far they had yielded only mind-numbing footage of shop doorways at night. The surrounding areas were combed, and combed again.

Police were also reassessing the statements taken concerning the murder of Sophie Bouchard, including those from the young people who had stayed at the Wilkommen hostel, in case they could find a person or incident to link the two. Both young women had stayed at the Wilkommen during their travels, but not at the same time, and there was no indication that they had known each other. People came and went at hostels, and very few left lasting impressions on the others.

The hostel itself had been thoroughly searched, to the discomfiture of its current residents and of Neil Connor, the caretaker. Hundreds of fingerprints and handprints had been lifted and were being processed; footprints were so indistinct as to be useless. Most, if not all, of the hostel's residents were young travellers. Some might still be in London, but many more would doubtless have moved on.

The autopsies of the bodies of Sophie Bouchard and of the most recent, unknown victim were subject to intense scrutiny. Hay had attended both autopsies himself, partly because it was his job and partly out of respect—if they had something to tell him he wanted to "hear" it first-hand. He had reviewed both autopsy reports numerous times, as well as hundreds of photographs of the crime scenes and of the bodies at autopsy. Clearly the photographers adhered to the credo of *the more, the better*.

DeJong and PC Joan Ryan had been detailed to look at possible links to other unsolved murders. With some misgivings, Hay also assigned officers to run checks on known sex offenders in the area. He thought this likely to be a dead end, given that the murders did not involve sexual assault, but he couldn't rule it out entirely.

Hay's thoughts returned to the similarity in the looks of the two victims. In his long career, he had never headed up an investigation into a serial killer. And yes, while three murders were required to designate someone "officially" a serial killer, there was little doubt in his mind that this was exactly what he was dealing with. He set aside the notion that one of the girl's deaths might have been used as a cover for the other: the important thing was that it appeared that the same person was the killer.

He had decided early in the investigation of the Bouchard murder not to publicize the existence of the mark on her hip. Now the second girl had a similar mark. The possibility that the second killing might have been committed by a copycat was remote. He didn't want to see a third victim. The only thing linking the two so far was their physical similarity. *So what*, he wondered, *if anything, is with the weight connection?*

A pale young man with blue eyes sat in a dingy cafe in East London, waiting for a burger. He thought the waitress looked dim—like someone his mother would have called a "drip." Which was, ironically, a good enough description of his mother.

The young man hadn't settled on another victim yet, but it certainly would not be this woman. She was middle-aged and scrawny, with a whiny voice and common accent. Her nails were gnawed and ragged. Eventually she flung the greasy burger onto the bar in front of him, along with some soggy chips, depositing the bill at the same time.

Definitely a class establishment, he thought wryly, slowly demolishing the burger and its trimmings before her impatient eyes. Finally he turned his attention to the bill. He waited for her to count out the exact change he was due, then headed out onto the damp pavement.

Although he had loved his sister Emma deeply, he didn't much like women in general. That dozy cow of a waitress was a typical example of the sex. Stupid and sluttish. Near-set eyes. Always a sign of ignorance. He pulled up the hood on his windbreaker and turned into a district of winding, narrow streets. The drizzle was turning into light rain.

His own mother, about whom he was again thinking,

had been a royal pain. When he came home from school she was either drunk or, as the years went by, had passed out long before he returned. He had always been far too embarrassed to have friends over. The thought of his mother filled him with revulsion: a flabby, blotchy woman with prominent broken blood vessels on her nose. At least she had had the good grace to support, in her own narcissistic, inebriated way, her daughter's modelling career.

His father he remembered only dimly. The memory was partial and blurred, involving a great deal of yellow light, and noise, and the sound of a man shouting. Sometimes this vague memory seemed to include the sounds of his sister crying. His father had passed out of the boy's life before he had turned three. The boy's mother never spoke of him again, even when asked direct questions by her son, who longed to know about the man who was his father. He remembered, once when he was an adolescent, her slurring the word "evil" under her breath, but then she went back to drinking her whisky and said no more. Not surprisingly, his own brief marriage had ended badly.

The blue-eyed young man had been to this area several times before, spending hours wandering the streets and wondering, again, about its most famous figure. As a child he had been both fascinated and disgusted by the stories of the Ripper, and had even invented a little saying that he found quite humorous during one of these visits: *once a serial killer, always a serial killer*. He chuckled again at his own cleverness. Thrusting his fists deep into his jacket pockets, he continued his private tour of the Ripper's Whitechapel.

EIGHT

Liz met the other students, the course director, and some of the instructors the following morning at breakfast in the dining hall at Bramshill. The hall was lovely. Some of the dark green paint was peeling, and erstwhile diners had scratched the heavy wooden table, but this only added to its charm. An ancient podium was stored against a long wall, presumably for speakers who wished to address the school as a whole.

She hadn't actually needed Hay to suggest that she skip the welcoming reception; she hadn't planned to go if she could avoid it, and her escort from the airport had told her it was definitely not a command performance. In fact, the driver told her she was the last of the international students to arrive, the others having arrived a day or two earlier. Presumably they had already managed to shake their own jet lag.

Liz, though, was fatigued. She decided she could only face some toast this morning. She poured herself two mugs of black coffee, almost finishing the first while waiting for the bread to pop up from an extraordinarily slow toaster. Always a bad traveller, she could happily have gone back to bed. Instead, she sat down by a small group of strangers in street clothes, assuming them to be her new colleagues since the rest of the hall was deserted. A few items of cutlery and a couple of mugs scattered about the other tables suggested there had been an earlier shift, probably, she thought, the police who were regular students of the college.

Her new colleagues comprised an American with a strong East Coast accent, two Australians, and a New Zealander. A couple of Brits involved with transnational criminal investigation were also in attendance. The only other woman was the New Zealander, a tall, dark-haired woman with a wide mouth, already involved in a friendly verbal spat with the Australians during the "full English" of bacon, eggs, mushrooms, tomatoes, toast, and coffee. One of the Aussies, a fit, blond officer, glanced over at Liz and smiled, then resumed bantering with the Kiwi.

After breakfast the group had a half-hour to themselves, and then the course began in earnest. The first module would address the future of DNA analysis, and soon Liz found herself fascinated by the subject and its potential for crime solving.

Hay already knew quite a lot about serial killers but only in a theoretical sense. He had never been involved in an investigation of that nature before. And while at present there were only two victims, the similarities—especially the physical similarity between the victims and the unusual mark on their hips—led him to believe that he could be dealing with this type of murderer. He wasn't about to leave this particular stone unturned.

Serial killers, according to his understanding, tended to be loners, frequently had substance abuse problems, and usually had suffered psychological or sexual abuse as children. They were often obsessed with power and control, and could be manipulative and charming. Early in their childhood, the killers' cruelty often manifested itself in maiming and torturing animals.

There was a myth that serial killers were highly intelligent. This was, Hay had learned, only a myth. Their intelligence was neither greater nor lower than that of the normal population. They blended into it, hence the oft-repeated sentiment of neighbours: "He seemed just a normal bloke."

Hay and de Jong met with a profiler to learn more. A psychologist with a professional interest in serial killers, June Nesbitt occasionally worked on contract with Scotland Yard. The middle-aged woman with wiry grey hair and narrow, rimless glasses met them in her office.

The surroundings struck Hay as deliberately devoid of any personal items. Not even a painting on the wall or a potted plant, let alone pictures of family members. Perhaps the nature of her work rendered her obsessively private.

Nesbitt rehearsed much of what Hay already knew, but added a few other personality traits common to serial killers. Then she rubbed an eye under her glasses and said, "Many of these killers have had some sort of traumatic head injury, such as a concussion. Some have suffered actual brain damage. Often there is some sort of trigger event that sends these people down their violent path. Not necessarily something that anyone else would find particularly distressing, but an event that makes a deep personal impression on someone predisposed to kill."

This information was fascinating and might eventually prove useful, but at the moment didn't shed a lot of light on his current cases. And Hay couldn't see himself going about asking suspects if they'd wet the bed after the age of twelve.

She stared at Hay, reproachfully, he thought. "Of course they are, by and large, men. Often prone to auto-eroticism, as well as violent sexual fantasies, voyeurism, and fetishism."

The profiler had seemed puzzled and, thought Hay, mildly disappointed that there had been no sexual element to the murders. Nor had she ever known a killer to target overweight women before. On this, however, she had a useful suggestion.

"Weight is becoming an area of increasingly specialized

study," she said, pushing her glasses back up her nose with a middle finger. "Some activists even describe fat as a 'feminist issue.' Most certainly agree that women are held up to unrealistic standards with respect to body image. Some become anorexic, some bulimic, some obese or morbidly obese. It is a rare woman who can look in the mirror and be satisfied with her weight. I don't know much about this, except from a personal standpoint."

De Jong was about to smile at her joke, stopping himself as he realized it wasn't meant as such. "But if you think it would be useful I have a contact . . ." She opened a thick leather folder in which she kept numerous business cards and began flipping through it. "Dr. Ira Herschell is a specialist in weight and weight-control issues. Here he is." She wrote out the contact information on a piece of paper and handed it to Hay.

This aspect of the case intrigued Hay. He thanked the profiler, carefully folded the note, and put it in his pocket. De Jong followed Hay out, deep in thought.

Jenny Ross struggled out of her recently acquired backpack and let it drop. It leaked rainwater onto the acrylic floor tiles of the hostel. Jenny was chilly, wet, hungry, and happier than she had been in her entire twenty-two years.

She had been born and raised in Lexington, Kentucky. Not the Lexington of sprawling horse farms, thoroughbred racing, and porticoed residences; rather, Jenny had grown up in an unkempt trailer park on the north side of the New Circle Road with her unemployed older brother and good-hearted but simple-minded mother. She wouldn't have recognized her father on the street.

Many people lay claim to an unhappy childhood, and Jenny could easily have done the same. Big, uncoordinated, and poor, she was picked last for school sports teams but was a great favourite among the school bullies. That she always had her nose in a book made her even more of a target. For Jenny, though, reading was a good escape from her tormentors, despite, or perhaps because, at her school, reading any more than you absolutely had to wasn't considered cool.

Not that she'd ever imagined she could be cool in the first place. But she did love to read, even though some of her classmates called her "Sigmund Freud" in a nasty way. She continued to be engrossed by her library books, re-emerging from them only reluctantly to face her actual surroundings.

Jenny began by reading romances but soon tired of their formula and moved on to more classic fiction. Then she turned to non-fiction, learning with fascination about far-off countries, their cultures and histories, their power struggles and battles.

She was very young when she realized that her mother was not only uneducated, but perhaps also had some underlying learning disability. Mrs. Ross was virtually illiterate and completely innumerate. She seemed to lack even the most basic common sense. Mrs. Ross wasn't able to cope on her own and depended on other people, including her son, Jesse, who was Jenny's older brother by three years. Mrs. Ross's own brother and a kind ex-boyfriend assisted her with the most basic of tasks. No one had ever thought of seeking help for the woman: she was just slow. Jenny began helping out with things like paying bills and writing cheques when she was about ten. She grew up quickly.

Jenny's brother, Jesse, was a good-natured young man completely lacking in ambition but quite happy to help his mother as required. He had taken over the cooking responsibilities in his early teens and, while he occasionally dabbled in drugs, his ham balls with sausage and deep-fried fritters were unrivalled. Jesse hadn't finished high school and made his living, such as it was, by doing odd jobs and dealing in small quantities of dope. He dealt only in small quantities because others further up the chain didn't think him responsible enough to provide him anything bigger than the odd small bag.

Although Jenny had learned much through applying herself to her books, she never considered going on to higher education, nor did her family or school expect her to. Graduating from high school was by itself seen as a major accomplishment. After graduation, she took a succession of low-paying, dull jobs, staying in the trailer park with her mother and Jesse.

In June of 1996, when she was eighteen, Jenny was watching a travel programme on television that described in exquisite detail the town of Xania on the Greek island of Crete. Suddenly she realized that she had no desire to live her entire life in the trailer and decided that, if nothing else, she would get out and see something of the world. Then she could settle back and stay home with her mother for good. Jesse could look after their mother by himself for a while.

So Jenny went back to a job she'd held part-time a couple of years earlier at a local fast-food restaurant. This time, however, instead of considering it a bore and a waste of time, she flung herself into it and worked as many hours as the chain could give her. She spent months flipping burgers, working late nights, and smelling like a deep-fat fryer. Slowly, even with her measly salary, she began to save money.

Jenny's permanently destitute mother, perhaps surprisingly, strongly supported her daughter's decision to travel, dimly recognizing that her own chance for such adventure had long since passed. Jesse said that sure, he would look after his mother, evincing no interest in travelling himself and vaguely wondering what on earth would inspire anyone to leave Lexington.

So slowly the money had accumulated, despite the occasional request from Jesse for a "loan." As Jesse was usually unemployed, Jenny had no difficulty in turning him down, knowing she would never be repaid. Jesse's response was typically just a slightly sad shrug of the shoulders.

When she wasn't working or taking care of her mother, Jenny continued to read avidly. European history, especially English history: the Wars of the Roses, the Reformation, the English Civil War. Before long her reading took a more practical turn: *England on $10.00 a Day* became a work of much study and planning.

Jenny continued to live at home. She saved money—enough for a return ticket to London plus some onward train travel on the continent; she also managed to put away a small amount for living expenses. Due to her hard work at the burger joint, Jenny was offered a supervisor's job if she stayed on. She was momentarily tempted but turned it down, refocusing on European travel.

Suddenly she was here, her backpack draining onto the floor of the hostel. A nervous-looking caretaker acknowledged her, and she was shown a comfortable bunk in which to sleep. A young German woman told her that the inn next door had long-lasting happy hours and good, cheap food. Jenny was too tired to eat, though, and was soon fast asleep.

NINE

Neil Connor, caretaker of the Wilkommen hostel, flopped into the faded armchair and looked, unseeing, about the tawdry flat. When his wife had told him they were finished earlier in the year, he had moved from Sheffield to London, into this tiny flat, unable to afford anything better. At least he'd found a job, though it wasn't much of one. Neil's wife, Betty, had kept the flat up north, which Neil knew was fitting: she was the only one making a decent wage anyway. Betty had called him "useless" and "without ambition," and he supposed she was right. Their marriage had lasted three years, but things had started to go downhill from the start.

It would have been nice to have someone to talk to now, though. Two murders at the hostel. Neil mechanically lit a cigarette, thinking about the evolving situation. He was uneasy, yet he had to admit there was some sort of eerie thrill to it. He turned the events over and over in his mind.

He could have done without that reporter lurking around though. Some skinny guy called Lombardy. Jake Lombardy. He had come to the Wilkommen twice, asking questions of all the travellers and asking him for the smallest of details. What the girls had looked like, what sort of personalities they had, how well Neil had known them. Lombardy was particularly interested in the investigation, asking Neil what sort of information the police were after and what Neil had told them. Lombardy was a pest. *Come to think of it, I don't even know what paper he's with. Even brought a damned photographer with him this time. Scrawny little bugger,* thought Neil annoyed, *taking dozens of pictures like he was on a modelling shoot.*

Not normally a man who read the papers, Neil had begun reading avidly about the murders—murders of girls he had seen. He couldn't recall any news items with Lombardy as a byline, not that he took much notice of bylines anyway. Neil glanced at the travel alarm clock on top of the small television and quickly reached for the remote. It was time for the news.

Dutch Inspector Gerrit de Jong had only been on secondment to Scotland Yard for a few weeks but had already found himself embroiled in the middle of a fascinating murder investigation. He had personally concluded early on that this was doubtless a serial killing, and that the killer wouldn't stop until he was arrested or killed. De Jong had kept his thoughts private, however. He wasn't here to rock the boat or to interfere with the methodical professionalism of the British police. His role, rather, was to build a closer relationship between his own KLPD and Scotland Yard.

The European Union was all very well, he thought, but some institutions, like national police forces, remained suspicious and sometimes jealous of other European forces. Information sharing among countries wasn't as good as it should be, and coordination and cooperation across jurisdictions—even within countries—was routinely troublesome.

De Jong had always been skeptical about the prospects for the EU in the first place, but as it was now a fait accompli, he had been pleased by the idea of a six-month secondment in London. His wife, Ilse, contending with two lively toddlers back in The Hague, had been less than impressed by this posting, and that lady was forming even less favourable views about the EU as time went on.

The Dutch Inspector was enjoying a Heineken at a noisy British pub, pleasantly aware that he was the subject of hushed conversation among some young women in a nearby booth. De Jong had not developed a taste for English beer, although there were many other things about the country he liked. The camaraderie and competence of his colleagues at Scotland Yard had impressed him. He had even heard favourably about DCI Hay while still in the Netherlands.

The fabled English countryside exceeded his expectations; and the food was not as bad as he had been led to expect.

De Jong glanced at his watch. It was 7:34 PM. He could go back to the office and see if he could lend a hand, but he'd already worked late and didn't want to look pushy. He was in a delicate position, well aware that he needed to be a team player and a diligent officer, but not come across as an interfering outsider. He could, of course, just go back to his modest hotel room. Neither of these options seemed especially appealing, so he ordered another beer instead, which seemed to please the young women in the nearby booth.

The exhibit at the small gallery in Pimlico was underway. Paul Rochon hadn't expected the new High Commissioner to put in an appearance, and his instincts were right. Somehow Roy didn't strike him as the cultural type.

Simon Simms didn't care, though—his first exhibition abroad was a dream come true. Even a reporter from a local arts magazine had come to take pictures. Simon thought the reporter looked a bit bored, but at least it was publicity.

The High Commission, he thought, had done an excellent job in staging the event. Some seventy people, including members of staff, contacts in the London arts community, and Canadians resident in London, were in attendance. Waiters floated about with hors d'oeuvres and glasses of wine. Simon couldn't eat anything, even though everything looked delicious. His stomach seemed to have shrunk to the size of a loonie. He did manage to swallow a couple of glasses of wine to fortify himself and calm his nerves. He smiled nervously around the room, wishing he could find someone to talk to, and was relieved to see Paul Rochon approaching. Rochon, privately annoyed that the guest of honour had been left to fend for himself—where was his Cultural Programme Head anyway?—shook Simms's hand warmly.

"I'm sorry the High Commissioner couldn't make it. He had a previous engagement," lied Paul. Of course, High Commissioner Lucien Roy had no such previous engagement. While doubtless Roy was still recovering from jet lag, Paul suspected he would need to cover for his new boss many more times in future. Paul inclined his head to summon Alec Shaunessey from the trade section in order to introduce him to Simms. Suddenly Paul saw DCI Hay, with whom he had become friendly during the investigation into the murder of Natalie Guévin, stride into the gallery. Paul made his excuses to Simms and Shaunessey, and stepped forward to greet Hay.

"Stephen," he said, extending his hand, "so good to see you. I thought you said you couldn't make it tonight?"

Shaking Rochon's hand, Hay replied, "I had to get away from the cases for a bit. Clear my head. So I thought I'd drop in for half an hour. Try to refocus."

Rochon nodded. "I'm glad you came." He flagged down a passing waiter and Hay smiled gratefully, selecting a glass of red.

"It's a Canadian Merlot, from a small estate in southern Ontario," Paul said, unthinkingly switching into official mode. "It's won two international awards, including Best Newcomer 1996." Paul stopped himself. "Sorry," he said.

Hay grinned and tasted the wine.

"It really is good," he said. "I don't often associate Canada with wine. Well, er, except perhaps ice wine."

"I hear that a lot," said Paul ruefully, "but we really are producing some world-class stuff." Hay made a mental note to sample some more Canadian vintages.

"Anyway, sorry," Paul said. "Sometimes I go on autopilot with the promo stuff. No progress, then, on the cases?"

Hay shook his head.

"A lot of leads, but so far none of them are going very far. We're doing everything we can to get to the bottom of the Bouchard murder." He wanted to reassure Rochon on that score, speculating, correctly as it happened, that Paul was getting some heat about the case from Ottawa. "And that of the other poor girl."

"Do you know who she is yet?"

Hay shook his head. "That makes it even more frustrating." He looked over at a painting on the wall next to them, which consisted solely of wide, colourful stripes with wavy lines running through them.

"Er, that's interesting," he muttered politely.

"Yes, isn't it?" agreed Paul, privately hating the painting and recalling the adage that diplomats were people sent abroad to lie for their country.

TEN

Late the following afternoon, DS Wilkins managed to detach himself from the eager DC Bell, sending him off in company of PC Etheridge to sift through the reports from the latest round of interviews.

"So, Wilkins, what have you got?" asked Hay, leaning back in his chair.

"A splitting headache," said Wilkins, collapsing into a chair across from the desk. "That new detective constable is doing my head in. He's following me around like a puppy, and I'm afraid he's going to ask me for a date."

Hay smiled. His DS seemed able to lighten the mood no matter what the circumstances—a trait that Hay, prone to gloom, valued. "And how's young Etheridge?"

"*That* one always looks as though he has a nasty smell under his nose."

Wilkins ran his hand over his thinning hair. "But what have we got? Not a great deal. Nobody's seen anything. The only guy who looked a bit nervy was the caretaker at the Wilkommen, but he did seem genuinely shaken when he saw the victim's photo. The interviews are being processed now, but none of them seem too promising. Any luck with an ID?"

Hay shook his head. "We're running the usual checks on missing persons, but nothing's come up. It's good to have the first name, but a surname would be a damn sight more useful."

Wilkins nodded. "It's all we could get. 'Susan.' With all the comings and goings at that hostel, we were lucky to get that much."

"And we don't even have anything close enough to try a dental comparison yet." Hay thought for a moment. "That caretaker—has he worked there long?"

"Just a few weeks, he said. He's moved down from Sheffield."

"Mustn't be much of a job."

"Didn't seem like much of an intellect. Probably all he could find."

Hay gazed out his window, asking almost automatically, "you're checking out his alibi?"

"Doesn't have one, really, but we're asking his neighbours if they can confirm he was at his flat on the night."

"Keep after it." said Hay. "He has opportunity."

Wilkins nodded, then paused and took a breath. He was now in unchartered waters. Hay was still looking out the window.

"By the way, Sir, I've heard from a friend of mine who teaches up at Bramshill that an Inspector Liz Forsyth from the RCMP has just arrived to take one of their courses."

"Yes, that's right."

Wilkins raised his eyebrows. "And I had to hear it on the street?"

"Sorry," muttered Hay, "must have slipped my mind."

Wilkins almost said, "as if" but valued his career too much, so just said, "well, say hello from me if you see her. And best regards to Ouellette."

Hay nodded, gazing into the dark street for some time after Wilkins left the office.

On Hay's instructions, Gerrit de Jong was reviewing ongoing and cold cases in the vicinity of London. The work was tedious and time-consuming, and it was already getting dark, but de Jong didn't mind, as it gave him a unique vantage point from which to observe the methods, workings, and structures of the Metropolitan Police. PC Joan Ryan had been assigned to assist; she had pre-cleared the files, sifting out the files of dead men, children, and cases of probable domestic violence.

De Jong worked from a cluttered desk in the open office space that was the headquarters of the murder squad. The room was noisy, the occasional sound of a shrilling telephone breaking the background hum of fingers rattling keyboards and officers consulting in muted tones. Occasionally laughter rang out: there had to be some release from the grisly business at hand.

He worked methodically through a large stack of files. While some of the information he sought had already been transferred to an electronic format, the complete files remained on paper. He had no intention of missing any details that some computer geek could have overlooked. Some marginal note made by an observant officer could be of significance. He moved some of the files to a small pile on the left side of the desk. When he had finished going through the larger pile, he turned his attention to the smaller, more select group of files.

Half an hour later he picked up two manila folders and headed for Hay's office.

"What's this then?" asked Hay.

"A couple of cases that might be of interest." Hay leaned back in his chair and listened.

"An unsolved murder from 1995," said de Jong, placing the first manila folder on the edge of Hay's desk. "A woman found dead, strangled, in Woking. Marnie Hollingsworth. Twenty-three, Caucasian. Left naked, off the path in a wooded area. Local force says there were plenty of leads but nothing new reported for at least a year."

"Anything about a mark on the body?" asked Hay, looking up from his desk.

"No."

"Weight?"

"Autopsy says 'well-nourished' but that could mean anything."

"All right," said Hay doubtfully. "What else?"

"Another woman found dead in Havering. There's not much on her, although Ryan's trying to get more details. Caucasian and young, violent sexual assault."

Hay sighed. "All right, follow them up. You can keep Ryan."

De Jong nodded and left the office.

ELEVEN

Jenny was, after all, on holiday. She might never have done this at home in Lexington but had decided to accept Drew's invitation for a drink. He seemed like a really nice guy, if perhaps a bit of a nerd. That was okay with her, though. Some people thought she was a nerd.

Anyway, it was interesting to meet new people and share experiences—wasn't that, in part, what this voyage was all about? So she agreed to meet him at a pub called the Three Compasses the following day at six-thirty. The pub wasn't far from her hostel, the Gateway.

She had initially bunked at a place called the Wilkommen on the recommendation of a friend back home but had found it a bit crowded and unclean. Then, when she heard about the recent murders of two previous residents, she moved on immediately. The Gateway was a bit nicer, and a little quieter.

Jenny had met Drew on her return from a coach tour to the Tower of London. The coach let her off some blocks from the Gateway, and, in a quite un-Jenny-like fashion, she began conversing with a young man whom at first she took for a traveller from the same hostel. It turned out that he wasn't a visitor; rather, he was a local trying to find a friend he thought was staying there. He asked her if she knew his friend, Eddie Fleming, but she hadn't met an Eddie. From there they fell into conversation, sitting on a decaying bench in front of the hostel, Drew tossing the odd cigarette butt onto the dirt and crushing it with his heel.

Jenny loved Drew's English accent, and he said he found her Kentucky drawl "charming." Drew wasn't particularly good-looking, and was on the skinny side, but she reminded herself that she didn't possess the ideal body type either. And the attention was flattering. Very flattering.

"What did you make of the Tower?" he asked.

"Wonderful," she replied. "I've read a lot of English history," she added with a sidelong glance, not knowing if he would be impressed by this or think her boring, like everybody else did. "So it's amazing to actually see the place where so many historical people were imprisoned. Beheaded even. Sort of brings history to life," she said, then cringed inwardly at the cliché.

But Drew agreed with her and related the story of the ravens in the Tower of London. Jenny already knew about the superstition—that if the ravens ever flew away from the tower, the Crown of England would fall—but she enjoyed hearing him tell the story and listened with rapt attention, pretending it was the first time she'd heard it.

Jenny found herself increasingly comfortable in the company of the shy, intelligent young man, so when Drew invited her for a drink it seemed natural to accept. Perhaps she wouldn't have done that at home, but this was England. Anyway, she couldn't get into much trouble in a pub.

Neil Connor, caretaker of the Wilkommen, pushed a stiff broom unhappily across the floor of the hostel. He'd just had another run-in with that reporter—that Lombardy fellow wearing his stupid fedora. The scrawny photographer was trailing after him, taking even more photos than before. He'd even taken pictures of the toilets with his expensive-looking camera. Lombardy assailed Neil again with the same questions he had asked on each previous occasion, and Neil provided him the same answers.

The entire affair had left Neil depressed—not that he particularly needed a reason to feel that way. Neil was often depressed—some doctor had called it "clinical depression," whatever that was supposed to mean. Since his wife had left him, he suffered more than before, and the murders—along with the police, the press, and the rubber-necked passers-by—had done nothing to improve his mood.

He was having a lot of trouble sleeping and even greater

difficulty getting up. His blue eyes were regularly shot through with exploded blood vessels, and the dark shadows underneath made him look older than his years. Fatigued, lethargic, and uninterested in everything, Neil sometimes thought about collecting his few possessions and moving away. Maybe he should never have come to London in the first place—he didn't much like it. But he couldn't go back to Sheffield either, knowing that he might run into her. Neil squeezed his eyes shut and turned his head away, as though from some invisible foe.

Then he opened them again and looked around. The hostel was vacant at present. It hadn't been so busy lately, and by early afternoon most of the young people were out in the city. He continued to sweep. The corner of the broom caught on the foot of one of the beds, and he suddenly became infuriated with this unexpected obstacle. He pulled violently on the broom, moving the bed a couple of inches in his effort to release it. Then he had to shove the bed back into position.

Somehow, between his tears and his rage, he went on with his work.

TWELVE

Liz made her way to the pub on the basement floor of the college. She heard the noise long before she found its source; the entrance was via a narrow, walnut-panelled corridor eventually opening onto a dimly lit room.

Liz's first reaction was to flee. She disliked large gatherings of any sort, especially when she knew no one. She was much lonelier in a large crowd than when on her own. But she had told her classmates she would join them and couldn't back out now.

Even when her eyes adjusted to the light, she saw no

one she recognized. She surmised that most of the punters, largely male and rather loud, were British police officers also taking classes at Bramshill. Soon, though, she was hailed by one of the international students, who steered her over to the table at which her fellows were seated. She sat on an uncomfortable wooden bench and gratefully accepted the offer of a beer from the American.

Liz was relieved to see that smoking was allowed in the pub and lit a cigarette, feeling a bit calmer with the first drag. She looked over at the bar, which had no stools but appeared to be propping up a great many police officers. Behind the bar were rows of pewter mugs.

"Oh, sorry," said Liz in reply to a question from the woman from New Zealand. "Yes, I think the course is great so far."

Inspector Melanie Craig from Christchurch was seated next to her, and they were soon deep in conversation about their respective jobs. In addition to their rank of inspector, the two women had much in common, including a liking for ham and pineapple pizza and old movies. Soon Liz was relaxing and enjoying herself.

The noise had ramped up another decibel or two when Liz decided it was her round, so she took the orders from her colleagues and went up to the bar. Pete Saunders, the blond Aussie, accompanied her to assist her in carrying the drinks. As they waited for the order to be filled, he asked, "So, Forsyth, married then?"

"No," replied Liz loudly, over the din.

"Living with someone, then. Engaged?" asked Pete, looking at her intently.

"Er, no. You ask a lot of questions."

"I'm a copper. That's what we do."

Liz laughed and they carried the drinks back to their table.

Liz had enjoyed the beer, though it was not typically her tipple of choice. In the pub at the Bramshill academy, however, it seemed to be if not mandatory, more than appropriate. At home she drank red wine, having begun her drinking career at university, with an unappetizing pink beverage whose name included the word "duck."

She had been attending the University of Calgary at the time, working towards a bachelor of arts in sociology. Liz had difficulty explaining, even to herself, why she had chosen to major in sociology. She could have selected any number of interesting majors, from English lit to political science, but the outcome would likely be the same: a good, general degree from which to consider the life decisions that open so many doors, and unexpectedly close even more. Her courses were interesting and she worked hard, coming away with excellent grades in her first year. During that time she discovered, among many other things, an enormous thirst for knowledge, more than she would have wished to know about the capriciousness of love and friendship, and a fondness for wine that did not have the word "duck" in its name.

Her second year was the revelation. Scanning the university calendar for optional courses, she settled on something called "Introduction to Criminology 201." She registered for this, along with another option on the theatre of Shakespeare and a mandatory science course (geography: she had never been confident about her abilities in science). Fascinated by the criminology course, she had switched her major to psychology by mid-year, concentrating on criminal psychology.

Her parents accepted this change with equanimity— after all, it didn't much matter what her degree was in, so long as it set her up with a decent job at the end. She was still working part-time in cosmetics at Sears and, between that job and her student loans, the family hadn't had to fork out excessive amounts of money to keep her at school.

When, having finished her final third-year exams, she announced she'd decided to apply for the police force, her father had been horrified and her mother privately delighted. The reverse was true when some time afterward she agreed to marry a handsome young man from the mens-wear department at Sears. Her father thought that marriage might settle his daughter down and keep her away from the perils of criminals and drug gangs and God knows what else, while her mother was quietly disappointed that her daugh-ter might not, after all, pursue the exciting career that she, herself, might have enjoyed.

When the marriage fell apart after about a year and a half, her mother was once again privately cheering her daughter on in her chosen profession. By this time, in the spring of 1980, Liz had been accepted by the Royal Canadian Mounted Police and was on her way to basic training in Regina. She never told her parents why her marriage had dissolved so quickly. Certainly much of it had to do with her career ambitions. Infidelity and violence would have summed it up handily, but the reasons didn't really matter at the time: it was just another failed marriage, and there were many of those about at the time.

"So it looks like a pretty packed programme," said Liz. She'd called Hay when she'd returned to her room from the pub. They had made an informal arrangement to talk each evening she was in England, if possible. "Maybe I could come down to London this Saturday and, uh, we could have dinner?"

"I'd love that," said Hay. "I wish I could come and get you, but my time really isn't my own at the moment. You know what it's like."

She did indeed, unfortunately. In the middle of a high-profile homicide investigation, let alone when it seemed a serial killer was on the loose, the chief investigating officer could hardly go swanning off to a country pub fifty or so miles away from the action. That Hay even thought he could manage a dinner out was flattering enough.

"I certainly do," she said, taking a long drag off her cigarette. Liz was back in her cozy room at Bramshill, watching the light fade over the surrounding fields as the distant forest darkened.

"Do you know how to get up here?"

"I'm hoping one of the constables will be able to take me. They've told us they will try to provide drivers if we want to go anywhere. If not, there's a pretty straightforward train route. Maybe you could pick me up at some convenient place? Once I find out where it is?"

"Of course," he said, and took another swig of black, bitter coffee. "There's a wonderful restaurant just off Hugh Street. French. At least I like it, and so does my sister-in-law Helena." He smiled, "she's lovely, Helena, but a dreadful food snob. I always take her recommendations." He wondered, but didn't really want to know, what his sister-in-law would say if she knew he was inviting Liz out for dinner. Helena had been trying to set him up for years with her own friends, acquaintances, and at times with women she scarcely knew.

They had all been nice enough, but Hay had felt like some poor horse at auction, bloodlines and conformation under scrutiny. He occasionally wondered if any of the women were going to verify his age by checking his teeth. Perhaps Helena had given up on him—she hadn't set up one of these introductions for some time. He shook his head quickly and refocused on the conversation.

"That sounds great," said Liz. "I'm looking forward to seeing you."

"And me." Just as the pause was about to become awkward, he asked her what she thought of her classes.

"First rate," she said. "The instructors, at least the ones so far, are very good and they've done a great job in putting the courses together. And this place is lovely. To imagine that it was once a home. Just amazing."

"So you're still doing the forensics course?"

"Mostly DNA. I tell you, when DNA analysis becomes fast and affordable, it will be an incredible asset to our work.

The criminals won't stand a chance." She added, "'Serial Killers' starts later this week."

"Already started down here," said Hay drily. "Anyway, I could use some help."

"I'll see what I can do." After a time they said goodbye, and each of them separately watched the evening turn black.

THIRTEEN

DCI Hay might have been irked, but unsurprised, to learn that his love life—or lack thereof—was the subject of conversation between his brother, Keith, and Keith's wife, Helena, at their home that evening. The couple had just settled in for their traditional pre-prandial martinis when Helena began, in her distinctively breathless voice, to pepper Keith with questions about his brother.

Keith occupied the sofa, and Helena sat nearby on a wing chair covered in coordinating fabric. Helena had taken great care in decorating her home and had turned it, in her own opinion, into a regular showpiece. She picked up her martini, admiring the pale pink of her carefully selected glassware.

"Poor Stephen, it must be absolutely horrible for him to have to look at dead bodies all the time and God knows what else he has to see every day—I don't know how he puts up with it and how he can just go home to an empty house after dealing with that all the time. It would drive me bonkers."

Keith took a sip of his excellent martini—long on vermouth, short on gin—and prepared for yet another homily by his beloved wife about how lonely his brother must be and how they must find him a mate. He settled back into the familiar depths of the sofa and inhaled deeply in anticipation.

"And it's not as if he's a weirdo or anything—he's a lovely, decent man with a good job who I'm sure has a lot to give to a woman, if he found the right one that is. God knows I've tried, Keith, I've really tried, but he's just impossible to set up with anyone." She paused, but only briefly. "Now Marta, I really thought she would be his type, but all he did that evening was swirl the wine in his glass, barely saying a word, and now I can hardly look her in the eye."

"Maybe he doesn't want to be set up," said the mild-mannered engineer.

"Well that's as may be, but it's not good for him and I worry about him, I really do." She took a large swig of her own drink.

"Maybe you should marry him yourself," said Keith, only

half joking at this point, although he did love his talkative wife very much.

"Oh do be serious, Keith. He's your brother after all—you should do something."

"Helena, I've told you time and again that if he wants to settle down with someone, it will be up to him, not us. He always was a loner, even at school." He took another slug of the martini. "You know that."

"Is he gay?"

"No, you know he's not gay. He was engaged to Paula before she was killed in that accident."

"Doesn't mean he's not gay," said Helena petulantly, gazing into her glass. "Some gay men get married. I've heard it happens all the time and then only years later the poor woman finds out the problem wasn't her after all."

Keith rolled his eyes. "Helena . . ."

"Well, it's not right. Just not right, mark my words. What about that Liz person anyway, that Canadian policeman—are they still in touch?"

"I think she would be a policewoman and, in fact, yes. I believe she's over here on some sort of training programme at the moment. Stephen mentioned it on the phone when we were talking last week." Keith tried to sound calm but realized quickly his oversight and knew he was in for a drubbing.

"*What?*" Helena's professionally shaped eyebrows disappeared somewhere into her hairline. "And you didn't see fit to tell me?" Infuriated, Helena took a large swig while glaring at her husband over the top of her glass.

"Well, er, it didn't seem important at the time," mumbled Keith, abashed.

"Not important? Not important! Well, then. With all the time I spend worrying about that brother of yours and you don't even tell me this Liz person is in the country and I could at least have had them over for dinner." Helena was already envisaging her candlelit table laden with crystal and silverware, herself modestly producing something exquisite from the kitchen to great praise all around.

"I don't think Stephen has time for dinners, Helena. He's up to his eyeballs in these murders. I don't even know if he's going to see her. At least he didn't say."

To Keith's relief, his latest comments allowed him a slight reprieve as Helena continued. "These murders, yes. What do *you* think? Both big girls apparently, according to the papers. Do you think that's why they were killed? I do. I mean, I don't *know* of course, but it would be an odd coincidence otherwise. But why would someone hate heavy women that much?"

Helena expected no answer to her barrage of rhetorical questions and Keith provided none. She arched her eyebrows at her husband.

"Did Stephen tell you anything about that during your conversation about the Canadian policewoman?"

"Of course not, dear. And we weren't having a conversation about the Canadian policewoman. Nor about his case, for that matter. You really shouldn't believe what you read in the papers anyway," he added, perhaps unwisely.

"Well I don't know how I'm meant to get any information

about anything if I don't. I'll probably have to read about that Liz person in the papers before I hear anything from you or your brother."

Once again overcome by her husband's monstrous lapse in sharing critical information, Helena banged her now-empty glass on her glass-topped coffee table and flounced into the kitchen to finish the veal scallops with mushrooms and cream.

Great, thought Paul. Not enough that I have a new High Commissioner to deal with. Now I have another inane questionnaire from Ottawa. He glared at the lengthy survey on his desk, clearly designed by some management consultant who knew nothing about government and less about foreign policy. *Seriously,* he thought, looking at the questions, *how many phone calls do I make in a day? How many do I receive? How many words do I write? How many meetings do I attend?* Headquarters had lately become preoccupied with engaging high-priced business consultants to tell Canadian diplomats how to do their jobs.

How many phone calls? he thought angrily. Did the actual *value* of the phone call matter at all to these people? How could a phone call postponing a staff meeting even remotely compare to a conversation with the Foreign and Commonwealth Office finalizing the agenda for the next G-7 summit? *How did you measure that?* he asked some imaginary, faceless consultant. (Paul acknowledged with some regret that the G-7 was morphing into a G-8 that would also include Russia, but that was hardly the point.)

Why did Headquarters insist on contracting these people and paying their exorbitant fees? These damned consultants did nothing but expound the latest fads in private sector management to a breathless public service. Somehow the art of diplomacy was supposed to be forced into the artificial confines of somebody's business model. Worse, senior management in the department—who should have known better—had evidently succumbed to the hype. Normally intelligent professionals, whose minds should have been devoted to foreign policy, were now to be heard spouting nonsense about "skill sets," "competencies," and "performance indicators."

Paul picked up the survey and stared at it in disgust. This was only the latest in a long catalogue of similar, time-consuming exercises. He stuffed it into the bottom of his already overflowing in-box. *What a waste of time*, he thought. And not just his. The same rubbish was doubtless hitting desks around the globe.

Paul, normally a mild-mannered man, if somewhat highly strung, rarely lost his temper. But this sort of thing made his blood boil. Elbows on his desk, he buried his face in his hands.

FOURTEEN

PC Etheridge and DC Bell walked into the large, open office space where the morning meetings of the murder squad were held. The team was almost fully assembled, it being almost 8:00 AM. Most of the squad members were sitting at desks, preparing to hear the latest developments and get their orders for the day.

Inspector de Jong was leaning against a radiator, seemingly in confidential conversation with DC Ryan. For some reason this annoyed Bell. *Doesn't she know he's married?* he thought with a flash of anger. *Or doesn't she care?* Bell held people to a very high standard of behaviour, particularly women. The two of them looked a bit too cozy for his liking.

DS Wilkins hung up the phone and, trying to contain his excitement, told Etheridge and Bell, whose eyes were still lingering on Ryan and de Jong, "We have an ID." Before they could elicit any more information, DCI Hay entered the room, which immediately fell silent. Wilkins quickly got up and spoke quietly to his boss, then Hay told the assembled officers to listen up.

"Her name was Susan Beck," said Wilkins to the hushed room. "Penicuik police just rang in."

"It's positive?" asked Hay.

Wilkins nodded. "Yes. The girl's parents saw the photograph on *CrimeWatch* and immediately contacted the police. They're on their way down now, but say they're one hundred percent certain."

"What else do we know?"

"She wasn't here for long. A week at most. She'd had an argument with her parents, which apparently wasn't unusual, and stormed out. She had apparently been talking about going to London for some time."

"Anything else?"

"She was twenty-one. That's all we have at the moment."

"All right. You know the drill," said Hay, turning his attention towards the room at large.

"Wilkins, interview the parents on arrival and offer all support. Find out as much as you can about her life and emotional state prior to her leaving for London. Her plans? Had she been in touch? When and how? Had her friends had any contact? Get me a timeline and let me know what I need to follow up on.

"Etheridge, get on to Penicuik and find out as much as you can about the girl. The usual: finances, friends, habits. Drugs, debts. Also," he added, nodding to a couple of other officers he had known for years, "try to find out if she knew or had any connection with Sophie Bouchard from Montreal."

"Apart from the initials."

Hay swung round to the source of this interjection, surprised to see young DC Bell blushing to the roots of his white-blond hair.

"Go on," said Hay.

PC Etheridge sniffed.

"Well," muttered Bell, "the initials are, er, the same . . . Sophie Bouchard, Susan Beck . . . just seems odd. Er, sorry."

Hay cast an appraising glance at Bell, then continued. "Make sure to find any commonalities or connections between the two, but don't invent any. Any luck on the cold cases?" he asked de Jong.

The Dutch officer shook his head. "Nothing. The two possibilities we had didn't pan out. The local constabulary is convinced theirs is a domestic. They don't have enough evidence to prosecute, yet, but that's where it's heading."

"And the second?"

"She was a prostitute, well known to local police. Looks like a client got angry. Clearly there was recent sexual activity, and it looked nasty. Seems to have involved a broken beer bottle. Forensics is working the DNA, but that will take forever. But no mark on the hip, no other physical similarities that indicate any connection to our guy."

Bell muttered that prozzies should expect that sort of thing, a comment that earned him a glare from PC Ryan.

Hay was checking his notes. "We've had preliminary results from forensics," he said. "As we suspected, both alcohol and Rohypnol were found in her system, and she was suffocated. No defensive wounds, no scrapings under the fingernails, no bruises, nothing. Nothing to imply sexual assault, although the pathologist was at pains to point out that sexual gratification doesn't necessarily involve intercourse." Despite his attempts to keep his features neutral, it was difficult for him to disguise the disgust he felt as he spoke.

Hay continued. "They did, however, find a tiny fibre on her"—he consulted his notes—"right cheek that matches the fibres found on Sophie's body. Acrylic, dyed grey. Get onto the forensics lab—we need to identify all possible sources and products." As he said this he nodded to a female detective, who had lately cultivated good contacts in forensics. "All right, let's go," he said. "We've got to find this guy, and fast. Not just because the brass and the press are all over it," he said, with a glance at a stack of newspapers on the press liaison officer's desk, "which of course they are. But we can't let this happen again."

As he said this, and as the squad began to file out, he remembered the words of Marie Bouchard, Sophie's mother, when he accompanied her to the airport along with the body of her murdered daughter. *You must catch this man*, she had said, *you must. No one could have hated Sophie.*

Hay had decided to call on the office of Dr. Ira Herschell, the specialist in bariatrics—the branch of medicine dealing with obesity—whom the profiler at the Met had recommended to him. Herschell's office was on Harley Street, and as Hay sought the address along the row of elegant facades, he speculated that the field of bariatrics must be a lucrative one. The address proved to be that of a charming, cream-coloured Georgian building, with a clean white archway and windowsills. A simple brass plaque announcing the name of the doctor hung from the imposing wrought-iron gate in front of the building.

Hay entered the private waiting room. Not a patient was in sight, and an almost oppressive silence hung over the room. As there appeared to be no one to whom he could announce his presence, Hay sat down in a comfortable wing chair and spent a few moments observing the tasteful furnishings and paintings in the room.

He was particularly taken by a small cameo in a weathered gold frame on the wall beside him, and wondered if it represented anyone in the doctor's background. Numerous healthy houseplants were scattered about the room, gracing what were evidently antique tables and bookshelves. A small number of the requisite out-of-date magazines lay in a neat pile on the low table in front of him. Presently Hay was greeted by an unsmiling, bespectacled woman with a very long nose, who identified herself as the doctor's personal secretary. He was conducted into the doctor's spacious office.

Dr. Ira Herschell was an unprepossessing man, short in stature and sporting thick, bushy eyebrows. DCI Hay explained that he was visiting on the off-chance that, because both victims had been overweight, their murders might be linked or possibly share a common motive. Herschell appeared somewhat taken aback but said that he would be happy to assist in any way possible.

"Do you mind if I call my assistant?" he asked. "He's fresh out of university and has read a lot of the current research as to why people become obese in the first place." He sighed. "My job is to try to correct things once the damage is done."

Hay agreed to the request and to the offer of tea. Herschell called in his assistant and then summoned the unsmiling woman; soon the tea things were on a small table at one side of the room near a lit fireplace. The men moved to sit there. The assistant had arrived, meanwhile—an eager-looking young man with a shock of light hair and wearing a white lab coat. Herschell introduced him as Dr. Morris Young.

"I realize this is all a bit vague," said Hay, adding a spoonful of sugar to his tea. "But I've always found it important to understand as much about the victim of a crime as possible. In some ways that's as important as understanding what makes the perpetrator tick."

Herschell nodded. "I can see that," he said. "Well, if you're wondering about obesity, and especially about obesity in women, it's actually a lot more complex than you might think. Yes, at its root, it's caused by consuming more calories than one expends. Period, full stop."

"But it's more than that," said Hay.

"Yes," said the doctor, stirring his tea and looking past Hay.

"It's driven by a combination of things, sometimes including poverty and lack of access to proper nutrition; sometimes ignorance of what foods lead to weight gain; sometimes by a need for instant gratification or as a means of dealing with pain or anxiety. Some in my profession choose to call it an 'addiction,' but I have some trouble with that definition."

He took a sip of tea and shifted his gaze back to Hay, who was listening attentively. What the doctor was saying was interesting, but so far Hay hadn't heard much that was surprising.

Dr. Herschell continued. "The entire problem has been exacerbated by specious advice from self-styled nutritionists. They've claimed for years that fat consumption equals weight gain."

"And it doesn't?" asked Hay, interested.

"It certainly provides gains for those pursuing research grants and for companies offering 'fat-free' options to a gullible public. But fat is essential to our diet. What's dangerous and fattening is sugar and carbohydrate. The ever-so-trendy 'low-fat options' are stuffed full of carbs and sugar in order to make them palatable. This is leading populations to become increasingly obese. It's all based on pseudo-science," he said with an angry shake of the head.

This made some sense to Hay. "So what our mothers told us was right? To lose weight cut out starches and dessert?"

Herschell laughed, if a bit bitterly.

"Exactly, Chief Inspector. You had a wise mother."

Hay agreed with that observation

"What about trauma, then?" he asked. "I've heard that

childhood or adolescent trauma or abuse can lead to eating disorders."

Herschell nodded slowly but looked doubtful. "Yes," he said, "that can be factor. And drugs used to treat trauma, especially antidepressants, can also lead to weight gain, which doesn't help the poor women already struggling with their weight."

The doctor again looked past Hay, gazing, unfocused, at a houseplant behind the DCI's shoulder.

"The fact remains, though, that women suffering trauma often turn to food. Why not alcohol, drugs, self-harm, any of the other behaviours so often associated with trauma? For these women it's always about the food."

Herschell paused and leaned forward, peering intently at Hay from beneath his wiry eyebrows.

"You see," the doctor said, "increasingly I see women who have just given up."

His assistant, who had taken no tea, nodded enthusiastically at his boss's last statement.

Herschell began to speak with greater determination. Hay wondered briefly if he was practising the delivery of a paper on the subject at a future medical conference.

"Women are fed a constant 'diet,' if you will, of images of women considered to be beautiful, desirable. Lovable. Because they're thin—very thin. A lot of women work extremely hard to achieve this so-called ideal. Very young girls and particularly adolescents fall prey to all sorts of fad diets. Some start abusing laxatives and force themselves to vomit, and some—the hard-core anorexics—stop eating altogether. There was one girl in here last week. Nine years old and already pretty far down that path."

Dr. Young nodded enthusiastically as his superior mentioned this. He had been fascinated by that case.

"What they don't realize," continued Herschell, "and what much of society doesn't realize—including the men who want their girlfriends to be thin—is that the number of calories a woman could consume to maintain this 'ideal' weight can barely sustain life. Such women are constantly hungry, constantly dieting, hating themselves and their bodies. So some of them just give up on the ideal, and turn to food. If they can't ever be considered 'beautiful' in today's world, they might as well enjoy the one thing that gives them pleasure—food.

"Food becomes both their number one enemy and their closest friend. An unhealthy, self-perpetuating cycle sets in, and the weight gain starts. Because their relationship with food has become so complex and dysfunctional, many are unable to deal with it and the weight just piles on. The ones who can afford it come here, or to places like this. I perform surgery, which occasionally, but to be honest not very often, affords long-term success."

The doctor's assistant, Morris Young, was shifting about in his seat, clearly wanting to add something. He struck Hay as almost excited. Herschell inclined his head, and Young, addressing Hay, said, "Did you realize that photos of even the thinnest of models are doctored to remove 'excess' skin on their bodies? So even the most 'ideal' of women aren't real anymore. These women are striving to attain a body type that doesn't even exist."

By the time Hay exited the building onto Harley Street, he found himself deeply saddened by what he had heard. He wasn't sure if this information would help him find the killer of these girls, but he was more than ever determined to bring the murderer to book.

Reporter Jake Lombardy emerged cautiously from behind a lamppost. He had followed Hay from the station to Harley Street. Was the DCI ill, or was he following some lead relating to the murders? He waited for Hay to disappear around the corner and then slouched up to the wrought-iron gate and read the brass plaque with interest.

FIFTEEN

Late that afternoon, DCI Hay and DS Wilkins were drinking weak coffee in the Battersea police station canteen.

"So, Sir, did this psychologist fellow have any ideas why someone would want to kill overweight women?"

"How would he know?" growled Hay. "He's the not the police. We are."

"I guess what I mean is, did he—or do we—have any idea why someone would hate big women so much as to want to kill them?"

Hay leaned back in the uncomfortable plastic chair, eyes still on his coffee cup.

"No idea. Of course, we're assuming he hates them."

"Er, yeah," said Wilkins in some frustration. Sometimes his boss was frustratingly obtuse, seemingly on purpose. "He does kill them. Not a sign of great affection, is it?"

With this, Wilkins bit into a pastry consisting largely of butter and sugar and somehow tasting of nothing.

"But think about it," said Hay, rubbing his arthritic knee. "Many serial killers pose their victims, often in offensive or shocking positions. The scenes can be violent, grotesque."

Wilkins's pastry tasted even worse than before and he put it back on his plate, wiping some powdery crumbs from his mouth.

Hay continued, "Our victims don't look like that. You yourself said that Sophie Bouchard didn't look dead at all, like she was just sleeping."

Wilkins nodded, remembering the apparent serenity of Sophie's body.

"So presumably these women are posed, but they look—well—pretty. A bit like sleeping marble statues," Hay said, thinking aloud. "No blood, no evident trauma, no signs of gratuitous violence."

"You mean then, Sir," said Wilkins, "that we're looking for someone who likes big women? But wants to kill them?"

Hay sighed heavily. That was roughly what he was thinking, but it didn't get them very far.

"What about the fibres?" asked Wilkins, switching back

to more familiar territory. "Was Watts able to get anything from forensics?"

"Yes and no. They were as helpful as they could be, but they weren't able to tell her much. We already knew the fibres on both bodies were the same. Cylindrical, dyed, possibly Asian in origin. Could be used for a number of products. Watts is chasing down possible suppliers and making an inventory of the sorts of products that include that type of fibre."

"And nothing else on the backpack?"

"No, just Beck's own fingerprints and some toiletries and a bit of clothing. God knows where the rest of her clothes got to. The stomach contents were interesting though."

Wilkins gave up on the pastry entirely and asked why they were interesting.

"Not so much what was in there," said Hay, "but the stage of digestion they were in. It appeared that Susan Beck had lunch the day of her murder, but no dinner. The time of death was during the night, so why didn't she eat? Was she abducted earlier? Or was she perhaps expecting to have dinner?"

Wilkins realized where the boss was going. "You mean she might have been expecting to have dinner with her killer."

"Exactly."

Hay looked gloomily at his coffee cup. "Check the Bouchard report. I remember more or less what she had eaten, but don't remember the time frame. Anything else from your side?"

"Just that we've got a few blurry partial footprints from the Beck scene. We're trying to match them, but it's tough going as they're just partials. It looks like he was wearing some sort of trainer." Wilkins sighed heavily. "And we know how many types of those there are."

Both men leaned back in their chairs. They knew all too well—at least to the nearest hundred—the number of such sports shoes currently on the market.

What a little shit, thought Geoffrey Hudson, carefully placing the camera in its imitation leather case onto his bookshelf. He was considering Jake Lombardy in this flattering light because, although he'd worked for Lombardy a few times over the last few weeks, Hudson still hadn't received a penny. The photographer walked into the kitchen of his rented flat to get a beer. Hudson had been offered some other work during the last couple of weeks, but Lombardy continued to insist he was "on to something" in relation to the killings and wanted to keep Hudson and his camera nearby. Lombardy had promised Hudson a daily fee and a cut of the major story that he was, he claimed, on the verge of breaking.

Hudson was young and deathly pale, even when in the best of health. He was attempting, with limited success, to grow a beard. Never much interested in school, Hudson's only talent was a slightly above-average ability to take photographs. For the past three years, therefore, he had eked out a meagre existence by taking pictures, supplemented by part-time work at a local camera shop, Photo-Phast. Sometimes, in lieu of wages, the shopkeeper "paid" him by allowing him to use their darkroom.

Hudson also made some money as a wedding photographer for bargain-basement weddings, and occasionally did photo shoots for awkward-looking families wearing frozen smiles. He had managed to sell a few photos to the tabloids, and dreamt, like everyone else in his profession, of that one shot that would make his career.

Meanwhile, though, he had to deal with people like Lombardy. Lombardy, he thought, was either genuinely onto something with respect to the murders or was a dreamer. Or possibly a con artist. Lombardy seemed sincere enough, though, claiming he would break details about the murders and scoop the rest of the press. Hudson was most curious to find out what Lombardy knew and decided to stick with the reporter, at least for a while longer.

SIXTEEN

Hay was back at his desk when the phone shrilled.

"Hay."

"It's a Luba Boswell, Sir," said the PC on the other end of the line. "She says she's a psychic, and that she's helping you with your investigations?" Hay thought he caught a smirk at the end of the PC's question.

That, thought Hay, *sounds like a job for Wilkins.*

DS Wilkins, immediately upon entering the crowded incident room, was hailed by a constable standing next to a desk with a telephone attached to his ear. The PC was holding the phone in his left hand and jabbing his right index finger repeatedly at the mouthpiece. He stared at Wilkins, eyes wide, eyebrows raised, and nodded once sharply. He was, thought Wilkins, exhibiting all the typical behaviours people use to convey that a phone call is for someone else.

Wilkins took the phone and was surprised to find the caretaker of the Wilkommen hostel, Neil Connor, at the other end of the line.

"You, er, gave me your card—t'other day—when you were here," stammered Connor.

"Yes, of course. Thanks for calling, Mr. Connor. What do you want to tell me?" Wilkins sat down in the desk chair just vacated by the constable and adopted his calmest manner; Connor sounded rattled.

Connor was indeed rattled, calling from the telephone box outside the hostel, eyes darting about to ensure no one was nearby. He took a deep breath.

"It's that reporter bloke as is always 'anging about. Calls himself Lombardy."

"What do you mean, always hanging about?" asked Wilkins, notepad at the ready.

"Don't know how many times he's showed up," said Connor. "Always asking about them girls. And about your lot and all. Seems as interested in what you're asking me as he is in finding out about them. Gets right up my nose."

"Would you like us to have a word, Mr. Connor?"

Connor's relief was physical. "Oh, yeah, yeah please," he said. "Would you? I can't get rid, and now he's bringing some photographer around with him and all. I don't know what he's after. He seems to know everything already anyway."

Wilkins talked to Connor a while longer, who provided further details about Lombardy's appearances at the Wilkommen. When the caretaker exited the phone box, he was much less troubled than he had been twenty minutes earlier. He smiled to himself in some satisfaction. That little journalist bastard would have to think twice before he started sniffing around the hostel again.

Liz had promised to phone her sergeant, Gilles Ouellette, back in Ottawa, to update him on her courses and get the latest from the office, particularly Ouellette's first impressions of the new superintendent, Murray Purcell. Purcell had assumed his new position about the same time Liz left for Bramshill, so she hadn't yet had the pleasure of meeting him. She remembered that one of the reasons she was at Bramshill in the first place was to give her a chance to think about whether she wanted to work with Purcell or look for a transfer. She'd hardly given the matter any thought so far.

Liz phoned Ouellette at his home following a quick lunch during Bramshill's hour-long lunch break. She wanted a frank discussion with him, which couldn't happen if her sergeant was already in the office, under the eye of his new superintendent.

"He's a bozo," said Ouellette. He had been about to leave for the office, but now sat down on a battered couch in his living room and kicked his feet up onto his coffee table. He was already wearing his boots, but the coffee table had long been accustomed to such abuse. Liz smiled. Ouellette had recently acquired the word "bozo" and employed it frequently.

"Could you be a bit more specific?"

"Well, just full of himself, you know. Seemed to take a dislike to me on sight—no idea why. Never smiles. Started quizzing me about you. I only told him good things, of course."

"Lucky for you," she said, smiling and taking a drag from her cigarette.

Ouellette continued his character description. "Likes to keep his door shut and his blinds down, and occasionally comes out to bark orders. He never even really introduced himself. We're all just keeping our heads down for the moment. But the atmosphere's already tense. I sure miss the old Super."

None of this came as a surprise to Liz. Purcell's reputation had preceded him.

"So how's DCI Hay?" Ouellette asked innocently. He and his opposite number, DS Wilkins, had noticed some electricity between their bosses when investigating the Guévin murder at the Canadian High Commission, although the two young sergeants were both too smart to have said anything, even to each other.

"Yes, fine, he seems fine. We've spoken on the phone. Of course he and Wilkins are up to their ears in these murders."

"Of course," agreed Ouellette. "Any other news about Wilkins?"

"Not much—just that he's still with Gemma. What's the weather like?"

Given that it was February in Ottawa, Ouellette's answer predictably included references to bitter cold, heavy snowfalls, and black ice, and Liz was pleased to again gaze upon the gentle, emerald landscape just outside her window at Bramshill.

"So tell me, how are the classes? Who are the other students?" The balance of the conversation dealt with these matters, and then Ouellette clumped out of his apartment to work; it was 8:25 AM. For Liz it was 1:25 PM, and she returned, thoughtfully, to class.

Unwittingly, Liz had provided Ouellette some misinformation. The previous evening, DS Richard Wilkins's long-suffering girlfriend, Gemma, had dumped him with little ceremony.

"It's not working, Richard, you know it isn't." She had looked at him steadily from under thick, curled eyelashes. "It's not you. It's the job. You're always working. Always preoccupied. You know you are. You have to be. It's your job, and you love it. But I can't take this anymore."

They were in Gemma's stylish Mayfair apartment—Gemma's father had a great deal of money and she had an excellent job—to which he had been summoned. Wilkins was slumped in a blue, patterned wing chair, looking like a condemned man. He tried to argue, plead, talk her out of it, and when she burst into tears he attempted, unsuccessfully, to comfort her. The problem was that he knew she was right. They both knew it. He left her flat and, wandering down the street a few moments later, realized some of his thoughts had already turned back to the serial killings. Yes, she had been right.

SEVENTEEN

"Okay, find Lombardy and send someone round to talk to him," said Hay to Wilkins, having been briefed about his sergeant's phone call from the Wilkommen caretaker. Hay looked at his sergeant, noticing the younger man looked strained and like he hadn't been sleeping well. "You all right?" he asked abruptly.

"Yes, Sir, fine," replied Wilkins, his voice a bit thick. "I'll go."

"Good," said Hay, knowing he could trust Wilkins's tact. "Suggest he lay off but make sure to tread lightly. Don't want some bloody headline about policeman plod telling the press what to do."

Wilkins nodded, preparing to leave, but Hay went on, "Maybe take Joan Ryan with you. Lombardy might take it better with a woman there. But it's interesting. This damned journalist has been around from the beginning, hasn't he? Going back to the scene of the crime, as it were. Even had the nerve to turn up at my office."

"Yes, you mentioned that. Do we know what paper he's with?"

"If I do, I don't remember. You know what I think of journalists."

Wilkins grinned. He knew full well what his boss thought of the "gentlemen of the press."

"You're sure you're okay?"

"Yes, Sir, just a bit tired."

"All right. Well, try to find out what you can on Lombardy. In fact," he said, "let's put a tail on him and find out what he gets up to when he's not harassing Connor. But discretion is the word with that one."

Even with the approachable and efficient DC Joan Ryan in tow, Wilkins's meeting with Lombardy hadn't gone very well. The journalist—or whatever he was—was leaving his flea-bitten flat just as Wilkins and Ryan arrived. He allowed them into the apartment, not inviting them to sit down.

As discretely as he could, Wilkins told Lombardy he was following up on a complaint, and suggested it might be best if the reporter steered clear of Neil Connor and the

Wilkommen for a while. Lombardy sunk heavily into a thread-bare grey couch, muttering, "Police are no help . . . have to get something somewhere." He was clearly annoyed and refused to make eye contact. Then he stood up, plainly indicating he wanted them out of his flat. He waited a few minutes, watching their departure from his window, then he left as well.

Having mobilized some of the murder squad to investigate Lombardy, Wilkins proceeded to fulfil another of Hay's instructions and so, once again, found himself in the elegant fifth-floor apartment of Luba Boswell—self-described clairvoyant, clairaudient, and clairsentient. She was as he had remembered her: spherical in shape, with plain features and a pleasant expression. Today she wore a bilious yellow twin-set and skirt.

Wilkins was alone on this visit. He sat down in an overstuffed armchair and declined the offer of tea. Hay had admonished him "not to waste too much bloody time" on the psychic. Luba Boswell perched opposite on a matching chair and studied the young man closely. He looked tired, she thought, with the beginnings of purplish shadows under his eyes. She remained silent for a few moments, then announced unexpectedly, "I'm sorry to intrude on your privacy, but this is good news. I think the woman I warned you about the last time is out of your life now?"

She tilted her head as she said this, and Wilkins looked at her, startled. He remembered very clearly that on his last visit to this apartment, Luba Boswell had warned him that a woman with a name like Ruby or Amber was "not the right one." He attempted to appear unruffled but found himself, atypically, lost for words.

"It's good," said Luba, nodding more to herself than to Wilkins. "Much better. Now," she continued, "the murders of the young women."

Wilkins regained his composure and began scribbling notes on his pad, although part of his mind was on Gemma and what the psychic had just told him. Luba continued to regard him, blinking slowly and at regular intervals.

She told Wilkins that the second girl, whom she had read was a Susan Beck of Penicuik, had not been as strong or smart as the first victim. She wasn't "coming through" in the same determined way that Sophie Bouchard had.

"She stands back, behind the first girl," said Luba, her eyes glazed now. "She is very shy and sad. But the first girl, Sophie, keeps telling me about her mother. She is so concerned about her mother."

Wilkins sighed, although not impolitely. He had heard this at their first meeting.

"She shows me newspapers. Newspapers with coloured photographs. Not local papers."

Luba drummed her fingers on the arm of her chair. "The colours are very bright," she said. "I don't know why she keeps showing me these newspapers. She is crying about her mother, poor girl," added Luba sadly.

"She's making me feel like she can't get any air. But she's woozy and can't breathe. Something is over her face."

Wilkins struggled to remember if the method of murder had made any of the papers, but couldn't be sure.

"I'm afraid that's all I can tell you," she said, "but I thought you ought to know. It might be helpful. Anyway, they are both close to crossing over, and I probably won't be able to talk to either of them for some time. They will have other things to do," she said with a happy smile.

"Er, thank you," said Wilkins, not sure what to think and feeling slightly woozy himself. There was something about talking to this woman that made him feel strange and disoriented. He thanked her again; they shook hands and he walked slowly to the elevator.

EIGHTEEN

Liz had enjoyed an intense but fascinating period of study, and spent one or two relaxing evenings in the Bramshill pub, during the first week of her course. Now— Saturday—was the day she would meet Stephen Hay for a long-awaited dinner. She almost wished he would call to cancel, saying he couldn't get away from work or something. Her nerves were on edge and she had a red spot on her nose.

Liz gazed unhappily into the mirror. At least she knew what she would wear—she had no choice, as she had decided what to pack back in Aylmer. Any second thoughts on that score were moot. But that didn't stop her from deciding one minute that her outfit was too casual and the next that it was too dressy. She gazed at the clothes on her bed, grumpy and convinced the ensemble would be wrong.

She applied some makeup, fluffed up her hair, and dressed in the now-detested black skirt and grey blazer, softened by a woolly grey, black, and green scarf. She slipped into her black heels and was ready forty minutes before she had to be. Liz sat on the side of her bed and looked out the window. She had quite a sharp pain in her gut—just nerves, no doubt, but uncomfortable nonetheless.

Liz had no idea what to expect. She had only met Hay in December, but he had been on her mind ever since. Her only comfort was imagining that he was feeling as anxious as she was.

After what seemed an excruciating wait, Pete Saunders, her Australian counterpart, knocked on her door.

"Hey, Forsyth, you ready?"

"Yes, yes, right there." She grabbed her purse and jacket and opened to door to Saunders. They went out to the waiting van together, where they met the American, all bound for London.

"Don't know why you don't want to come out with us," said Saunders. "Allan here," he said, indicating the American, "knows all the best places. At least that's what he tells me."

Allan smiled. "Not necessarily all the best. Just some really good wine bars and a couple of jazz clubs. It's great to have transport," he said, smiling at the youthful man who had been assigned to take his charges to London and get them safely back.

"I have no doubt you two will have a great time," said Liz with a grin. "Wouldn't want to cramp your style, though, would I?"

"You don't know what you'll be missing," said Saunders, opening the side door with a flourish.

"I might not want to know," she said, clambering into the vehicle.

"So what is it anyway—you got a date or something?" asked Pete curiously as they were settling into the seats.

"Something," said Liz. She wasn't being coy; even she didn't know what it was. Pete surveyed her with interest.

Charles Barraclough (PC, retired) was acting as driver for the international students that evening. He had volunteered to do the same every Saturday and Sunday evening during the course. Still in his early thirties, Barraclough had been injured early in his career by a rifle shot; his active policing days had been over in an instant.

He received a good pension but occasionally did some volunteer work for the Met and was part of Motor Pool Transport. He'd jumped at the Bramshill driving job when it came up. Essentially, it was a good excuse to get out of the house. His wife, pregnant for the first time, was consumed by culinary cravings at all times of the day and night. Now that her sister was staying with them, he could both absent himself and make some money as well. Driving a gaggle of foreign coppers around was nothing compared with trying to find *gulab juman* at 3:00 AM. No, this was a good gig and he was happy to have it. He turned onto the M4 and headed for London.

Over an hour later, due to surprisingly light traffic, Barraclough pulled the van into the drive fronting the luxurious Hilton on Park Lane, from which he would pick up his charges again at 12:30 AM. The Hilton was a convenient spot for him to drop them off and pick them up, and comfortable surroundings if any of them had to wait.

"Better make sure you're back here at 12:30 sharp," Barraclough warned his passengers with a grin. "None of you could afford to spend the night in this place unless you're paid a damn sight more than our lot."

Having assured the retired constable that they would on no account be late, the three international students exited the van. Liz had some difficulty as the vehicle was quite high off the ground and one of her shoes almost fell off, but Saunders handed her down gallantly. She waved the men goodbye as they headed off to explore their wine bars and jazz clubs.

Retired PC Barraclough drove off to amuse himself in London as best he could in the meantime, although he wasn't sure he would have much fun. For obvious reasons he couldn't go for a pint.

Liz was left alone in the lobby of the Hilton to panic a bit about the evening ahead. She almost wished she could just hit the town with her Australian and American colleagues, but Hay was due shortly.

He would turn up right on schedule, of course, but Liz had been cooling her heels in the opulent lobby and fretting for at least ten minutes prior to his arrival. She sat down and stood back up numerous times. She checked her lipstick twice in the small mirror in her purse, in case it should be smeared or, worse, stuck to her front teeth. A few men cast interested looks in her direction, and she briefly hoped she didn't look like a high-priced prostitute in this pricey hotel.

Hay was here, though, but not driving the Rover she remembered so well from her previous visit to London. That had been in December, when they had jointly investigated the Guévin murder at the Canadian High Commission. It was only February now, but suddenly the investigation seemed a very long time ago.

This time he had prudently taken a London cab, as one thing Hay knew he had in common with Liz Forsyth was a love of red wine. He got out of the cab and had a quick word with the driver, who kept the motor running but stayed put. Hay was even taller than she had remembered. And she noted again how straight he stood, elegant in an unselfconscious way. For his part, Hay didn't recall her being quite so beautiful. And she was wearing a very chic outfit.

There is considerable confusion, across borders and on both sides of the Atlantic, about how many kisses it is appropriate to plant on the cheek of a friend, and in which order these should occur. In some places, such as England, one is usually considered adequate. The affectionate natures of Poland require at least three kisses, often followed by a kiss to the back of the hand. Whether in multiple-kissing cultures one starts with the left cheek and goes left-right-left, or begins with the right to go right-left-right has puzzled many, and has led to some exceptionally embarrassing events.

Regrettably, this source of international consternation arose during the very first moment of their meeting. In approaching one another, each sadly mistook the other's intention and, after a couple of poorly targeted kisses, ended up kissing one another smack on the lips. It had been the intention of neither participant and was by no means what either of them would have seen as the ideal first kiss. But it was done, and done very badly, and a frazzled DCI Hay opened the cab door to a highly coloured Inspector Forsyth.

NINETEEN

Jenny was at the Three Compasses at 6:30 PM sharp. In fact she was there at 6:27 PM, according to the wall clock, totally undermining her efforts not to appear too anxious. Drew was late, not by much, but enough time had elapsed to give Jenny the sickening feeling that she might have been stood up. At the moment, she believed herself to be the only woman to ever have experienced that particular feeling. Then he was there, sliding into the seat across from her and apologizing—something about an unexpected phone call. He asked her what she wanted to drink, then went to the bar to get her a bourbon and Coke and himself a beer.

She looked around the pub, which she hadn't done earlier due to her anxiety that Drew might not turn up. It was nice, she thought, leaning back into the booth and feeling ineffably more relaxed. Not too noisy, but enough customers to make it comfortable. It was dimly lit, with old-fashioned prints of dogs and horses on the walls. Some men were playing darts at the other end of the room. There were coasters on the table in front of her, advertising a type of beer she hadn't heard of before. It was all strange yet familiar at the same time. This looked exactly how she imagined a pub in England to look. And here she was, and a nice English guy was buying her a drink.

Three young men were downing pints at the bar. They had each glanced at Jenny but looked away as quickly. Had they taken the time, they would have noticed that Jenny Ross had a perfect, clear complexion, glossy dark hair, and an open, intelligent manner. They didn't notice any of that, although one of the men—the youngest, at eighteen—tried to catch her eye. He had heard somewhere that fat girls were easy and wondered if this were true. She didn't return his glance, and he went back to discussing the division final.

Jenny smiled happily as Drew returned with their drinks, and noticed what nice blue eyes he had.

Jenny was starting to feel a bit light-headed. She was confused by this, as she'd only had one bourbon and Coke, and she could typically put away far more bourbon—even straight—than that. Drew was up at the bar, ordering another round of drinks. She smiled to herself when she saw he'd left his backpack on the seat; why on earth had he brought a backpack on a date? Maybe he really was as much of a nerd as she was. Drew turned back to her and grinned as he waited at the crowded bar. Jenny smiled back. *He really is pretty cute*, she thought.

She had never had a boyfriend before. Some boys who were friends, but she'd never been on an actual date. *Maybe*, she thought, *that's why the drink has gone to my head so quickly.* But she made a mental note to slow down a bit. Or perhaps they should order something to eat.

When Drew returned to the booth with the drinks, she mentioned that she was a little hungry.

"Oh, we're not going to eat here," said Drew with a smile. "I want to take you somewhere much nicer than this for dinner. It's fine that we started here because it's convenient for you, but I've a really good Italian place in mind, not far from here. Oh—you do like Italian, don't you?" he asked, instantly nervous.

Jenny found his sudden discomfiture quite endearing and quickly reassured him that yes, Italian was her favourite.

"My brother, Jesse," she said, "cooks really well—mostly Southern food—but he makes a really good lasagna."

Drew relaxed. "You'll like this place then. Do you like to cook?"

"A bit," she said, "not so much, but I can make a few simple things. Jesse's the gourmet."

Drew smiled. "You're not drinking," he said.

"Oh, sorry," replied Jenny, taking another sip. "Seems to be going to my head pretty fast tonight."

She smiled shyly and took another sip to be polite. Her head was, though, spinning a little, and some internal alarm told her something wasn't quite right. But her thinking was a bit muddled. He really was very good-looking—and good company, too.

The noise in the room ratcheted up a couple of decibels, and they had to speak quite loudly to understand one another. Drew was telling her about a recent tour he had taken of Whitechapel, following the route of the Ripper murders. Jenny was fascinated and said she would like to do that tour as well.

"I can take you if you like," he said. There was an earnestness about him that Jenny found disarming. "Maybe tomorrow, or the day after?"

"I'd love to," she replied, excited at the prospect of another date—a second! She felt quite euphoric at the prospect of an actual relationship with a young Englishman.

"Of course, I've read all about the murders—who hasn't?" she said. "And there are a ton of theories out there, but nobody seems to have a solution. I mean, there's, um, Tumblety . . ." She tried to remember the names of other suspects, gazing at her drink, but her memory was a bit foggy. "And . . . Lechmere." She could remember no more, which puzzled her a little. Her memory was almost photographic at times. Jenny shook her head, perplexed by the possible identity of the Ripper, as well as by her own lapse of memory. She looked up. "Do you think they'll ever find out who did it?"

"Maybe," said Drew. "I imagine it gets more difficult every year that passes. More speculation and decreasing forensic evidence."

Jenny found this a very intelligent assessment and sipped again from her glass.

"So," he said, "I have to go the little boy's room. How about you finish up that drink and we head off for dinner?"

"Sounds great." As he made his way through the crowd to the washroom, Jenny looked dubiously at her still half-full glass. When she was sure that no one was looking, she carefully poured it out under the table into a corner of the already littered floor. She didn't want to get drunk and make a fool of herself—not when she wanted to make a good impression. She was really starting to like this guy.

The restaurant, Chez Patrice, was small and exquisite. The lights were low, and the pale-yellow walls turned to amber in the candlelight. White linen napkins contrasted with dark blue tablecloths. Three large, gilt-edged mirrors adorned the walls, as did numerous quality prints of Impressionist paintings. In the centre of the room, an enormous arrangement of flowers rendered most of the tables quite private. Liz found it tastefully appointed; Edith Piaf belted out her classic repertoire, her exuberant voice muted by the sound system.

"You mentioned Piaf during one of our earlier meetings," said Hay softly. Liz smiled, remembering she had made some joke about his not regretting "rien" at a pub during their earlier investigation.

The elegant maître d' ushered Liz and Hay to a corner table, providing yet more privacy, and the wine list, menus, and ice water were produced quickly and smoothly.

"This is gorgeous, Stephen."

"Yes," said Hay, looking around. Liz had, of course, been offered the best seat by the maître d'; she sat with her back to the wall and was able to see most of the room. Hay's view was only of Liz, although he was able to look sideways. Moreover, one of the mirrors was behind Liz, so he was able to take in the room at a glance.

"You've been here before?"

"Just once," he said, "with my brother and his wife for a birthday or something. Keith and Helena are regular customers, though."

"I know you mentioned your sister-in-law, Helena, once before, but I don't know anything about the rest of your family."

She had pulled a cigarette from her pack and while Hay was quick with his lighter, the maître d', well versed in such matters, sprang into action and lit her cigarette with lightning speed. Then he lit Hay's and said their waiter would be with them shortly.

Sometime later, Hay had selected a Côtes du Rhône and their waiter had described, in appetizing detail, the night's specials. (The soup du jour was consommé à la Normandy and the crepe of the day was spinach and Camembert. The mains included duck à l'orange, lamb shank with haricots and red wine mushroom sauce, and poached sole with almonds and lemon, alongside pavé du patates.)

The specials, in combination with the à la carte menu, clearly meant deciding what to order would take some time. But this was definitely "French service" and they were not about to be hustled along. This suited them both. Finally, they were able to have a conversation about the sorts of things people usually talk about on a first date, even though they had already known one another for over two months now.

This is actually starting to feel like a date, thought Liz, as she looked into his face. He was talking about his family and his boyhood, which is what she had intended. She had learned a few things over the years, and one of them was that men liked to talk about themselves. So the occasional question elicited quite a lot of information from DCI Hay, while allowing them to become more comfortable with one another.

Hay wasn't altogether unaware of this technique, however.

"So, Forsyth," he said, reverting to the use of her surname. "Am I being interviewed for a serious crime or just a minor misdemeanour?"

She laughed, almost choking on her cigarette.

"I'm sorry, Stephen. Force of habit. I'm not awfully good at small talk so I find the Socratic method easiest."

Hay smiled and took a sip of the wine.

"I know what you mean. Anyway, now you know all about my family. Your turn."

The waiter, who had been observing them for a while,

sidled up to the table to take their orders for the first course. With the wisdom of his fifteen years in service, he thought it looked like a first date. He also thought it appeared to be going extremely well.

They ordered the hors d'oeuvres (pear and walnut salad for Liz, the crepe of the day for Hay) and settled in. By now there was no need for investigative techniques or dating savoir faire—they were both having a wonderful time, and neither noticed when other customers finished their meals, paid their bills, and went out into the wet London night.

TWENTY

Drew had told Jenny they would take a shortcut to the Italian restaurant, but it didn't seem particularly short. They had walked for some time along an unkempt pathway and she was starting to feel weak.

"Just a little bit farther," he coaxed. "There's a bench just at the end of this path, and you can sit there and catch your breath."

Jenny was again puzzled. She could normally walk for a very long time.

A bench did, in fact, appear, and Jenny collapsed onto it,

fatigued. The bench was hidden among a stand of very tall trees, at the edge of what looked like a park.

"I'm sorry," she said. "I don't know what's wrong with me tonight. How much farther is the restaurant?"

"Not far. But look, take a drink of this," he said, producing a flask from his backpack.

"Oh, no, really, I've had enough."

"Go on. Just to fortify you on our way to the restaurant." He glanced at his watch. "We have time before our reservation."

"You made a reservation?" she asked.

"I'm sorry if that sounds presumptuous. I'd hoped you'd have dinner with me."

She smiled, happy and dazed, and took a swig of the proffered flask.

"What is this?" she asked, trying not to wrinkle her nose.

"Just scotch," he said. "Sorry I don't have any bourbon with me."

Jenny was about to say that was fine, but found herself slurring her words a bit.

"You do know that you're very beautiful, don't you?" Drew had seated himself next to her on the bench. He reached his arm around her.

She tried to say, "do you think so" but whatever words she spoke were distorted and unfamiliar. Suddenly she found herself sitting on the ground in front of the bench, and Drew was kissing her and trying to undo the buttons of her blouse.

"Drew," she tried to say, "Drew, what are you doing? Drew?"

"Don't worry. I'm not going to hurt you," he murmured quietly as he kissed her again on the mouth and reached down to unhook her jeans. "You're just so damn beautiful. Everybody needs to see how beautiful you are."

Jenny understood what he was saying only vaguely.

"I just can't help myself," he said.

Jenny didn't understand what was happening, not really, but when she felt herself having difficulty breathing—something was blocking her airway—she began to thrash about on the ground and tried to release her wrists from whatever was holding them down. She was suddenly overcome with a fury she had never felt in her life. She was angry at something, someone, she wasn't even sure what, but she was enraged. She even had a strange, fleeting thought about this being her hard-fought visit and that she wasn't giving it up for anything.

A dose of adrenalin and an instinct for survival began to overtake the drug she had unwittingly ingested. Wielding her full strength and terrified bulk, she shoved her attacker violently aside, and somehow staggered to her feet. Drew had been knocked onto his back but was now sitting on the ground, recoiling in fear. He gazed at her in shock.

"No," he said, eyes wide with fear. "What are you doing?"

This hadn't happened to him before. The other girls had been quiescent, drugged, asleep. He wasn't prepared to deal with a woman who was not only conscious, but also panic-stricken and angry. He stared at her in amazement for a moment.

Then he grabbed his backpack and fled into the trees.

Somehow Jenny managed to pull her top back on and grab her bag. Then she saw that there was some sort of cushion on the ground. It looked like one of those things people put around their necks in airplanes to make themselves more comfortable. She grabbed that too and stumbled towards what sounded like distant road noise.

The appetizers had been wonderful, although the food probably could have been pretty lousy and they would still have had a great time. Prior to the arrival of the lamb shanks, which they had both ordered, they began discussing Liz's course at Bramshill, with which she was extremely impressed.

"I think the Aussie was hoping I'd come along with them tonight," she offered.

"What makes you think that?"

"Oh, he's just been, sort of, paying me a bit of attention."

"Women often think that," said Hay, as this had been his experience in policing. He had come across a lot of women who thought they were quite irresistible, on the flimsiest of grounds.

"Oh," said Liz a bit stiffly.

"Oh, no, sorry. Gawd. Not what I meant," he said. "Of course he would find you attractive. Who wouldn't?"

The lamb arrived at that moment, which was opportune and gave them both a chance to recover.

"So," said Hay, in an effort to get things back on track, "you're doing serial killers now?"

The waiter had been about to fill up the water glasses but danced backward to avoid the table upon hearing this question. Oblivious to the waiter's movements, she replied, "Mmmf," having taken a first bite of the melt-in-the-mouth lamb. Eventually they were able to manage both the meal and the conversation, and Liz told him of the interesting official from the Met, and the psychologist, who were jointly giving the course on serial killers.

"It's covering a lot of the well-known ones, starting, of course, with your Ripper."

"*My* Ripper?" inquired Hay, as the waiter again sidled into the background with his water jug, thinking this sounded like one of the odder first dates he had ever presided over.

"Well," said Liz, "perhaps not *yours* exactly, but the focus is on the English killers for obvious reasons. Working on the similarities and patterns common to most of them. Quite fascinating really, everything from brain injuries to abusive parents, from methods of operation to their leaving behind their 'signatures.'"

"Signatures," mused Hay. He had heard of this before. Some killers posed bodies in similar positions when they left the crime scene; some took the same sorts of items with them from every victim; others cut off pieces of hair or other "souvenirs" to look at later and relive the crime.

"Yes," said Liz, "I even heard of one case where the killer removed the victims' eyeballs."

At this, the waiter gave up and decided if they wanted any more water, they could bloody well get it themselves.

When the dessert menus were produced, Liz declined, noting, "I really can't. I have to watch it."

This interested Hay, who immediately responded, "Are you worried about your weight, then?"

As soon as the words were out of his mouth he thought, *Gawd, twice? Have I already offended this woman twice in one evening?*

Before he had a chance to apologize for his gaffe and somehow explain why he had put such an indelicate question, Liz began to laugh. She had quickly understood why he was asking and put him out of his misery.

"Well, of course," she said, smiling, "most women tend to be."

Hay looked at her intently. "Do you think I'm right in thinking the weight angle has something to do with these murders, then?"

"I do," she said. "Absolutely."

A frantic young woman bolted into the police station. A couple of drug dealers and a prostitute regarded her with mild interest as she stumbled up to the duty officer station and burst into hysterical sobs.

Liz allowed herself to be talked into sharing a chocolate mousse with Hay. It was luscious and airy, with supremes of orange infused with Grand Marnier on top. Hay was telling her about the limited forensic evidence found at the two crime scenes, including the backpack that had evidently belonged to Susan Beck. The fingerprints on the pack had matched Susan's, and the items inside were essentially toiletries and a few pieces of clothing. What had happened to whatever clothing she might have been wearing before her murder was unknown.

They were making good progress on the mousse, cheerfully bickering about who could have the last bite, when Hay's phone rang. A couple of other diners shot Hay disapproving looks, but the call didn't last for long.

"I'm so sorry, Liz, but I have to go."

She was disappointed but could only guess it had been a call from the station.

"Another victim. Looks like it could be the same attacker, but this time the girl got away. I have to see her right away." He signalled the waiter, who reluctantly approached the table.

"Of course," said Liz. "Let me get this."

"Absolutely not," said Hay, producing a credit card and handing it to the waiter even before receiving the bill. "And I'll pay for you to get a taxi back to the Hilton. I hope you won't have to wait too long there for your ride?"

"No, not at all," Liz lied. "The PC from Bramshill is supposed to be picking us up around 11:00 PM, so I'll only have to wait a half hour or so." In fact, the PC wouldn't be picking her up until around 12:30 AM, so she would be hanging about the hotel lobby for some time. She hardly needed to remind herself that this was part and parcel of being a police officer.

Hay quickly paid the bill, apologizing several times, and they went out into the cool, humid night to await taxis to their separate locations. A couple of black cabs pulled up and Liz was about to thank Hay for a wonderful dinner, when he took her face between both his hands and kissed her, hard, on the mouth. This time it was on purpose.

TWENTY-ONE

Deputy High Commissioner Paul Rochon was at home, making his way through a short stack of articles about the European Union, attempting to assess what sort of impact this evolving institution would have on Canada-UK relations. During the past couple of weeks he had spoken with several people in the Foreign and Commonwealth Office on the subject, as well as with a number of local academics and businessmen. He found the subject fascinating and it was one of his pet issues—one that he thought Ottawa needed to stay abreast of. But when he realized he had read the same paragraph three times without absorbing a word, he placed his latest article on the coffee table and removed his reading glasses.

It was just after nine o'clock at night and Paul's mind was actually on the phone call he'd received from Ottawa earlier that evening. As expected, his posting to London was to be terminated. The two senior positions at the High Commission in London—both the High Commissioner and his deputy—were now occupied by francophones. The new High Commissioner, party hack Lucien Roy, was a French Canadian, as was Paul. This did not constitute a proper balance, and it was Paul who would have to move on.

He took a swig of his scotch. The BBC News was on television, but he had muted it so he could concentrate on his reading. At least Headquarters was trying to be fair. Paul's personnel officer knew that London had been his dream posting and that it had been a very difficult one to date. Now he was being forced out after only two years. Paul had been offered a choice between returning to Ottawa as Assistant Deputy Minister for Security and Intelligence, or cross-posted to The Hague as Ambassador to the Netherlands. These were both plum assignments, and he knew that anyone from his intake year would be thrilled to be offered one of them, let alone both. He knew himself well enough to know that he would eventually become excited about whichever assignment, but at the moment all he felt was disappointment. Paul loved London. He had been an anglophile his whole life, despite having grown up in Quebec City and briefly, as a youth, nurturing separatist sentiments. He delighted in the English countryside, was fascinated by English history, and couldn't get enough English literature. *Odd*, he thought, *that I have to leave because I'm a francophone.* Of course, he saw the rationale in this—it would be equally preposterous to have two Anglos occupying the top spots at the Embassy in Paris.

He had met many people he liked here, too. Made some actual friends, including Stephen Hay of the Yard. Paul didn't make friends easily, but there were a handful of people here he would very much want to stay in touch with.

Lucien Roy, the new High Commissioner, was not one of them. Roy could have been worse, Paul reckoned, but he was damnably lazy. Paul had had to convince him that yes, it was necessary for him to make an official call on the British Foreign Secretary, yes, he did have to accept the invitation to a dinner in honour of the visiting Head of State of Sweden, and yes, he was expected to host a reception for a well-known Canadian *chanteuse*. Thus far it appeared that Roy either didn't get it or didn't want to. He liked going around with the Canadian flag flying from the aerial of the official vehicle, though. And he seemed to enjoy tormenting the High Commission chef with all manner of quirky meal requests. Poor Carillo had more than once been compelled to call Paul to have him explain what butter tarts were and where he was supposed to find potted pork.

Paul shook his head. His own successor hadn't yet been named, and the transition wouldn't take place until the summer. The usual sense of dread came over him as he thought about the need to update his inventory of belongings, take pictures of some new acquisitions for insurance purposes, deal with the inconveniences of packing, moving, and living out of a suitcase—all the time-consuming minutiae of moving, yet again.

Despite these annoyances, he wouldn't be sorry to see the last of Roy. It was, in fact, starting to look as though the next couple of years in his position might be as troublesome as the first two. The Hague, thought Paul, was looking better all the time.

TWENTY-TWO

Jenny had agreed to undergo a sexual assault kit. She'd told the police she hadn't been raped but was anxious that Drew be found and punished; she was willing to do anything that might help in his capture. She was taken to a local medical centre, where a sympathetic nurse took some blood for analysis, and where she was examined for other possible evidence. The tests were quick but thorough.

She had also agreed to return to the station to be interviewed by the officer in charge, who was on his way. She had nowhere to go anyway. She was afraid to return to the hostel. Drew knew where she was staying. Jenny cried for a while in the back of the squad car, but her tears had dried when they drew up in front of the station.

In a bleak interview room at the police station, Jenny was given a cup of tea, milk, and two sugars. A female officer was posted outside the door and checked on her from time to time. Soon Jenny was joined by a pleasant-looking young man who introduced himself as Detective Sergeant Wilkins. She agreed to a second cup of tea, and Wilkins apologized for her wait. His boss, he said, was coming in from the western part of London and would be there as soon as possible. They didn't speak much, but Jenny was comforted by the presence of the young man, feeling safe for the first time in hours.

About ten minutes later she heard some bustling outside the door and it opened again, this time to admit a tall, white-haired man who introduced himself as Detective Chief Inspector Hay. He, too, apologized sincerely for her wait, mumbling something about heavy traffic, and thanked her for her cooperation. Pulling up a chair, Hay observed the distraught yet self-possessed young woman at the other end of the table. Her long, dark hair looked wild and tangled, contrasting sharply with her pale, broad face. Her wide-set eyes, hazel-green in colour, gave him the impression of a highly intelligent cat.

"Would you like more tea?" asked Hay gently. "Or something to eat? You've had a long wait."

Jenny shook her head. Food was the last thing on her mind, and she felt she was already swimming in tea.

"No, thank you. Maybe later. But I want to help. This

guy's really dangerous." Hay noticed the soft accent of the American South. Her voice was monotone but not unpleasant.

Hay nodded, partly in agreement, partly in encouragement. "How did you first meet him, then?"

Jenny explained that she had met the young man calling himself Drew upon her return to the Gateway hostel following a coach tour of the Tower of London. Without prompting, she provided as accurate a description as she could.

Wilkins was taking notes quickly, briefly wishing all witnesses were as seemingly reliable as this young American.

"About my height, five nine-ish. Probably around 150 pounds, or less. He was pretty skinny. Called himself Drew. No," she said, catching a look from the young sergeant, "I didn't get a last name." She thought for a moment. "Weird, eh?" she said, addressing Hay. "I would never have done that at home."

She continued. "White. Washed-out looking. Bad skin. Not very good-looking at all, I guess," she said with a dry laugh. She remembered that a few hours earlier she had found him attractive, and fleetingly wondered if all women sometimes allowed themselves such delusions.

Jenny focused her eyes at a point on the opposite wall, thinking hard.

"He had a funny accent. English, sort of 'BBC' I guess you call it here. I thought it was nice. But . . ."

Hay inclined his head.

"Well, it sort of *slipped* from time to time. Some words sounded more like he perhaps wasn't as—what do you say here?—'posh' as he wanted to sound."

"Did you ask him about it?"

"No, no." Jenny shook her head at her own folly. "I wanted to make a good impression. Anyway, it was no big deal. I don't know a whole lot about accents so I could have been wrong."

"Can you remember anything else?"

"Not really," she said. "I started feeling woozy while we were in the pub. We were supposed to be going for dinner. He was buying me bourbon and Coke, but I chucked one of them away under the table when he wasn't looking. I was getting so light-headed. I can usually hold my liquor. Then we started walking to this restaurant. Supposed to be a good Italian." She looked up in some surprise. "I guess there is no such place." It was more a statement than a question, and she twitched her head at her own folly.

Jenny went on to describe the attack and her escape, how she had grabbed the "neck cushion thing"—she didn't know why—and had managed to flag a car on a nearby roadway and get to the station. She spoke very matter-of-factly.

"That took a lot of guts, to get into a strange vehicle after what had just happened," said Wilkins.

"I suppose it did," she said, momentarily taken aback. "I was still pretty light-headed and maybe in shock or something. I couldn't think of anything else to do." Her intelligent cat eyes, now bloodshot and half-closed, swung back to Hay.

"I'm really tired now. Can I sleep in a cell or something?"

They had done better than a "cell or something." Jenny was taken to an uninhabited, furnished flat with some basic

148

foodstuffs and a promise that the female PC, or another one, would stay with her. Jenny stumbled onto the bed and fell asleep within moments.

Hay returned home to Pimlico. Exhausted, he had quickly knocked back a couple of scotches to unwind but was unable to sleep. He looked at his digital clock and saw that it was 2:04 AM. By reflex he calculated the time difference between here and Ottawa, then remembered that Forsyth wasn't that far away at all, and that, before he had been called in to interview Jenny Ross, he had been having a wonderful dinner with the lovely Liz Forsyth. On that thought, he was finally able to fall into a light sleep.

TWENTY-THREE

Liz got back to Bramshill at about one-thirty in the morning, accompanied by her Australian and American colleagues. They had evidently had a great evening, and smelled of whisky, talking a mile a minute and occasionally bursting into song. Liz was more subdued, and, having replied that she too had enjoyed a good evening, laid her head back on the headrest. Former PC Barraclough, the driver, was very tired and looking forward to some sleep, all the while worried that he might wake his wife when he got home and be commissioned to deliver some pistachio yoghurt.

When Liz returned to her room, she quickly got ready for bed and fell asleep, dreaming vividly. Hay, in one dream, had grown very fat, and Liz told him he shouldn't have had that chocolate mousse. Then she was being pursued by someone she was convinced was a serial killer, although at times he looked a good deal like Pete Saunders, her handsome Australian colleague. Despite the intensity of her dreams, she slept soundly.

But she found herself bothered by something at breakfast, and it took all of the food and three-quarters of a large pot of coffee to realize what it was. Something about Hay's case. Something she had learned at Bramshill. She finished her coffee, wondering if she might be letting her imagination run away with her. She decided to call Hay.

The morning meeting of the murder squad was more than usually fraught, with the new information about, and from, Jenny Ross adding impetus to an already fervid investigation. A sketch artist had worked on a sketch based on Jenny's description and was meeting Jenny that morning to work on the finer details. The young woman was still exhausted, but as willing as ever to help.

DS Wilkins provided the information he had learned about Jake Lombardy. Lombardy had very little money and less work. He picked up freelance work whenever he could—which was apparently not often. Wilkins and some of his colleagues had phoned their own contacts in the press; no one had heard of a Jake Lombardy. He had apparently only been in London a short time, having moved from

Telford the previous November. But the previous evening he had stayed in his flat from five-thirty onward, so he had no connection to the attack on Jenny Ross.

Suddenly there was a timid knock on the door, and a gangly, bespectacled young man entered the room carrying a folder full of photocopies of a sketch. The room fell silent as the photocopies of the face of a young man were passed around. They looked in silence at the face of the killer.

"We don't want to frighten him off," Hay told the officers. "If he's not already fled or in hiding, he will be as soon as his ugly mug appears in the tabloids or on TV. Let's give it a day or two anyway. Meanwhile, check out the hostels, the Wilkommen and the Gateway. Get in touch with the families of the previous victims, Sophie Bouchard's mother and Susan Beck's—see if they've seen this guy. Ditto with the residents of the council estate next to the place Bouchard was killed, and the shops and flats close to the Beck killing. Get that picture out to the airports and railway stations and tell them to apprehend on sight. But no press. Not just yet."

DS Wilkins kept his thoughts to himself, although he wasn't sure that he was in complete agreement with his boss about this—surely he didn't still think Lombardy might be connected? PC Etheridge was wondering when the meeting would be over, as he needed to find a toilet.

Andrew Bell, however, screwed up his courage to tell Hay that he had been doing some research on Rohypnol. Among other things, the young DC had learned that the drug could cause amnesia or partial amnesia. Hay took this information on board, but it was the last thing he wanted to hear. He would need Jenny's testimony and, if they found the killer, it would need to stand up in court.

Hay returned to his office, his mind still buzzing with the latest on the investigation, and a bit preoccupied by the sketch, which he had seen for the first time at the morning meeting. The face it portrayed looked vaguely familiar to him, but he was unable to place it.

Wilkins had buttonholed him after the meeting to tell him that he had been right: Sophie Bouchard hadn't eaten dinner either on the evening of her murder. So the MO, thought Hay, appeared identical. The killer invited the women out for an innocent drink, and offered them dinner. Only they never reached a restaurant.

Hay realized suddenly that he hadn't asked Jenny if she wanted to contact the US Embassy. She hadn't suggested doing so and it hadn't occurred to him at the time, but he had learned that consular services were there to help nationals who had run into trouble abroad. He thought that he should mention this to Jenny, although she struck him as a woman who wouldn't ask for help unless it was absolutely necessary.

His phone rang. It was Liz. Her voice was a welcome relief, especially as she was telling him how much she had enjoyed their evening, despite its abrupt denouement. But quickly she changed tack.

"I've been thinking," she said.

"Really," he said. "What a surprise."

She laughed. She was sitting in her room at Bramshill and working on her third coffee. She'd lit a cigarette before dialling.

"No, seriously," she continued. "I've been thinking about your case. Remember how we were talking about serial killers having 'signatures'?"

"Of course," he said.

"Well," she said, "I could be way off base here, but I guess between the course and our conversation I'm spending an unhealthy amount of time thinking about serial killers. That segment runs through Wednesday, by the way," she said, stalling for time as she suddenly wondered if she was overstepping the mark. She was in fact, about to offer her thoughts to the investigating officer, of another force yet.

Hay had no such compunctions and immediately asked her what she was thinking. There were a lot of things he didn't know about Liz Forsyth, but he did know she was an excellent detective.

"Well," she said a bit hesitantly, "I was wondering if the mark this killer leaves on the hips of his victims could be, well, a signature. Like we were discussing, but literally a signature. Like, say, an artist, signing his work? Do you have any artists in the frame, so to speak?"

Suddenly Hay remembered where he had seen the face in the sketch before. He thanked Liz and hung up, then wasted no time in putting a call through to Paul Rochon at the Canadian High Commission. Paul removed his glasses and answered in his usual weary, lightly accented tones.

"Stephen? Great to hear from you. How are you?"

"Fine," said Hay, "and unfortunately I'm calling on business. This is a long shot, but I'm just wondering if that young Canadian artist—you know, the one who had that little show I came to—is still around? What was his name again?"

TWENTY-FOUR

"Uh," said Rochon, thinking quickly. "Simms. Simon Simms is his name. And no, I don't know if he's still in London or not. I can probably find out from Consular though. Or maybe the Cultural section"

"Would you please. As I say, it's a long shot, but it's rather—er—delicate, so if you could find out as tactfully as possible I'd appreciate it."

Paul grinned. "I'm a diplomat. I'm supposed to be tactful."

"And here's me, a policeman, who's meant to be anything but. Talk about coals to Newcastle."

Paul laughed. "I'll let you know as soon as I find out." Paul hung up the phone, looking down at the papers before him, which he had been studying prior to Hay's call. It was a draft list of potential invitees to a dinner to be hosted by fledgling High Commissioner Lucien Roy, which had been put together by a member of the political staff. Paul recalled the horror on Roy's face when confronted by the necessity of hosting such an affair at the Official Residence. It appeared that the prospect of hosting an auspicious gathering of diplomats and senior British officials in his new home filled Roy with dread. Paul had been forced to insist that this needed to be done if the High Commissioner were to make the right contacts and project Canada as an international player. *It's not just riding about with the flag flying on the car and enjoying the perks*, Paul had thought at the time, although of course said nothing. He was glad he'd be out of here soon, though. His earlier reticence about leaving his "dream posting" had evaporated early on in his dealings with Roy, and now he wondered how soon he could be cross-posted.

Later in the day he had a meeting with what were still colloquially known as the "friendlies"—Embassy representatives from a handful of European countries, Australia, New Zealand, and the United States—in order to discuss the latest crisis in the European Union. He had numerous reports to review and sign off on, a debriefing on a potential commercial deal, plus a reception that evening. Paul checked his watch and realized he could spare a couple of minutes to try to discover the whereabouts of the young artist of such interest to Hay.

It was Sarah Farell, Head of the High Commission's Cultural Programme, who furnished Paul with some useful information. She had a local phone number, but not an address, for Simms, although she didn't know if he was still in the country. Paul called Hay to pass on the information.

Hay ordered DC Ryan to ring and to feign a wrong number if a man answered. He did. *Still here, then*, thought Hay. He had the number traced to an address in East Acton. *Now*, he thought, lighting a cigarette and leaning back in his office chair, *we have to get to this guy without making him spook and run back to Canada.*

Of course he was by no means sure this was the right guy, but he was indeed an artist, and well worth talking to. Anyway, Hay had a secret weapon—a survivor by the name of Jenny Ross.

TWENTY-FIVE

Jenny had been sitting in the back seat of an unmarked police car for just over two hours, gazing at a rundown apartment building in an impoverished corner of London. This was a side of the great city that she couldn't have expected to see when planning her trip. The buildings had, perhaps, been attractive in bygone days, but they now appeared tumbledown and forlorn. Many had boarded-up windows, and paint was peeling from window frames and doorways. She noticed one wooden door on a seemingly abandoned house across the street:

it hung lopsidedly from rusty hinges, threatening to crash onto the front step.

Jenny had come to trust DCI Hay, currently occupying the passenger seat. He had interviewed her on that terrible night just a couple of days ago and, in subsequent meetings, she had concluded that he was a decent man. He was the first policeman she had ever really spoken to. Occasionally, at home, burly officers dressed in black and brandishing handguns would visit the trailer park late at night to break up fights or, sometimes, look for drugs. But she hadn't spoken with any of them, nor had she any cause to.

Hay didn't have a gun, so far as Jenny could tell. Moreover, he'd managed to make her feel comfortable following her ordeal. She had without hesitation agreed to try to identify her attacker and would stay in London for a while to do so. She hadn't known what to do next or where to go anyway. Now she was glad she hadn't just fled back to Lexington.

She shifted uncomfortably in the seat. The car smelled a bit unpleasant—some disagreeable combination of leather and tobacco, rubber, and possibly old sandwiches. There wasn't a lot of legroom in the back, and she was trying to keep her head low. She didn't want to be seen by her attacker if she could avoid it, despite her determination to have him arrested.

She had called home earlier to talk to her mother and older brother, and lied convincingly to both about what had happened. As far as they knew, Jenny was having a wonderful time on her European journey; they boasted regularly of her travels back at the trailer park.

Her brother, Jesse, in particular, admired his sister's

gumption and her willingness to travel to exotic places. He was proud of how smart she was—she seemed to be able to discuss any subject with a degree of knowledge and confidence that he didn't share—and, while he never understood her desire to go far from the bluegrass state, he was always happy to hear of her adventures. Of her current situation, however, he knew nothing.

DS Wilkins was in the driver's seat, directly in front of her. From Jenny's vantage point it was hard not to notice that the younger man was balding, while the senior officer had a nice head of thick, white hair. Jenny didn't know that a couple of the people wandering around the neighbourhood were actually undercover police, planted in the vicinity in case the suspect realized what was up and tried to leg it.

Despite the strain of waiting for the possible killer to make an appearance, Hay, Wilkins, and Jenny were all becoming a little bit bored. It was a raw, blustery day, the sky spitting fat drops of rain every now and again. It was quite cold in the car and, although Jenny had been provided a woollen blanket, she occasionally shuddered.

Hay and Wilkins were discussing some people she didn't know: one called Forsyth and the other called Ouellette, which she heard as "wallet." The DS was asking Hay if he'd seen anything of Forsyth; Hay seemed to deflect this query by asking a question of his own about somebody called "Gemma." Jenny was left to reflect on who Wallet and Gemma might be, when she caught sight of a slim figure in a camel-coloured coat, collar turned up at the neck and sporting a long, plaid scarf.

TWENTY-SIX

The man was exiting the building they were watching.

Hay heard Jenny gasp.

"Jenny?"

There was silence from the back seat.

"Jenny?" said Hay with greater urgency, half turning to look at the young woman. She had turned deathly white. She said nothing.

"Is it him?"

Jenny was terrified. She wanted to run but didn't want to leave the safety of the car. Her breath was quick and shallow, and she gulped for air as she remembered, through a haze, the night she had last seen the man who was now sauntering down the street.

"Jenny," said Hay with a calm he didn't feel. "Tell us. Is that the man who attacked you?"

It wasn't as easy as Jenny had expected it to be. She hadn't thought she would feel so frightened, so vulnerable. She looked at Hay, now looking directly at her. She nodded almost imperceptibly, trying to inhale.

"Tell me, Jenny, is it him?"

She nodded with more certainty now.

"Yes," she said. "It's him. Drew."

"You're absolutely sure?"

"Absolutely." She felt she was about to vomit.

Simon Simms sat in an uncomfortable plastic chair in an interview room at the police station. He was alone. A tape recorder sat on a shelf on the wall. Simms knew that a guard was stationed outside and suspected a camera was hidden somewhere. He had been there for about twenty minutes and hadn't been offered any tea. He could have used some tea.

Simms had known it would come to this, but he hadn't expected it to happen so quickly. That Jenny girl must have had something to do with it, but he didn't understand how he could have been identified and found so quickly. He worried that his message about the dead women might not have been understood; he had really needed more time.

Simon thought about his sister, Emma, who had killed

herself when her modelling career had ended abruptly. He often thought about Emma. *Lost her job, took her life*, he chanted to himself. And the alcoholic slut who had been his mother. He drummed his fingers on the table in front of him, and thought with some regret about his own career as an artist. He'd known for a long time that his stuff wasn't especially good, even though the Canada Council apparently thought he had some talent. He wondered what would happen now. Would he be tried and imprisoned here or sent back to Canada? He was curious about this but relatively unconcerned. He'd known it would happen sooner or later.

Simon recognized the two men who had arrested him and were now entering the room, accompanied by a snooty-looking uniformed officer who remained by the door. Simon noted with relief that the younger man carried a tray upon which balanced three Styrofoam cups and some packages of sugar and containers of milk. He accepted a cup gratefully. Wilkins turned on the tape recorder.

Hay and Wilkins studied the young man in silence as he added large quantities of sugar to his tea. Hay looked steadily at the thin, quiet man before him. He had seen him before, of course, in the guise of a young painter from somewhere in Ontario, for whom the Canadian High Commission had helped organize a small exhibition.

Simon Simms, whom Jenny had known as "Drew," had ash-blond hair and very pale blue eyes. He blinked infrequently. His skin was badly pockmarked. His nose was a little too large for his face and his ears stood out, not simply because they actually stuck out from the side of his head, giving him a slightly simian aspect, but also because they were bright pink, contrasting oddly with the rest of his face. Wilkins thought Simms's eyes so very light in colour—almost fading into the whites of his eyes—that the young man reminded him of something out of one of those dreadful horror movies Gemma insisted on seeing.

Simms wore a green T-shirt with "Edmonton Eskimos" in gold lettering on the front, faded blue jeans, and some sort of trainers. PC Etheridge, arms akimbo and standing stiffly at his post inside the door, wondered idly what Edmonton Eskimos might be.

Wilkins took out his pen and notebook and made a note to remember to confiscate the trainers at the end of the interview. He waited for his boss to begin.

Hay, waiting for Simms to finish fixing his tea and look up, had a folder in front of him from which he produced three photographs: one of Sophie Bouchard, one of Susan Beck, and one of Jenny Ross.

"Do you know these women?" Hay asked abruptly.

"Yes," said Simms calmly. "Two of them I killed and the third one—that one," he said, pointing at the recent photo of Jenny, "got away." He took a sip of tea, but it was scalding hot so he put it back down.

Wilkins, surprised, scribbled "holy shit" in his notepad.

"And why did you kill them?" Hay's surprise was almost as great as the sergeant's.

"You don't know?" said Simms, shocked and disappointed. "You don't understand? None of you?" He looked from Hay to Wilkins to Etheridge at his post by the door.

Etheridge simply shook his head disdainfully and watched the wall.

"So there was no point after all?" Simms appeared shocked—the first time he had exhibited any real emotion during the interview so far. Hay watched him closely. Simms had initially looked surprised and then disappointed, but these emotions quickly gave way to fury. The young man jumped up out of his chair, upsetting his tea, and began shouting that they were all "idiots," "clowns," and "bastards." Wilkins stood up quickly, and he and Etheridge sat the painter back down again, hard. He struggled against them for a while, occasionally shouting out a new insulting epithet for the police, but eventually he calmed down, his eyes cast downward. Hay continued quietly to study him. The PC stayed behind Simms's chair, and Wilkins returned to the other side of the table.

"We were meant to understand something, then, and we didn't tumble to it," said Hay softly. "Is that right?"

Simms nodded sullenly.

Hay took a guess. "Were we supposed to recognize the beauty of the dead women?"

Simms slowly raised his pale eyes and a look of relief came over his face.

"You do understand," he murmured.

"Not entirely," said Hay. "Why did you have to kill them?"

"Well of course I had to kill them," said Simms impatiently. "People just looking at them on the street would either ignore them or just dismiss them as fat."

"So you killed them because you wanted the police to see them?"

"Not the police. Not the bloody police," said Simms, exasperated. "Everybody. I wanted everybody to see them. I wanted everyone to understand how very beautiful real women are." He paused. "Not those stick figures strutting down the runways."

"And why did you care so much about that?" asked Hay softly.

Simms was momentarily confused, somehow having expected the white-haired DCI to have, by now, understood everything. Then he told them. About Emma. The modelling, the pills, her career, her suicide. It took him some time, and the police listened in silence until he concluded his story.

"You should have seen her, Chief Inspector," said Simms. "She was the most beautiful creature on this earth. Look—I have a picture." He paused. "Oh, no, they made me give them my wallet and stuff before they put me in here."

He paused. "But she really was gorgeous. Until they got a hold of her. The modelling companies. The agents were worst of all. They killed her, you know. They did. She took the pills, yes, but they drove her to it."

"When did you come up with the idea to kill these young women?"

Simms explained that he'd been harbouring a few vague ideas for months, but suddenly things had come together during his January visit to London. He'd come on a holiday with two of his artist friends from Ontario, and during that time they had attended the exhibit by Saskatchewan-born artist Louise Chapman. Hay nodded, remembering dimly seeing three young men leaving the exhibit, which he, too, had visited at the invitation of Paul Rochon.

Simms explained that one day while he and his friends were riding the bus, he had noticed a young woman sitting across from him, gazing out the window. She had reminded him powerfully of Emma, except that she was heavy. She looked like a larger version of Emma, and he thought her very beautiful. To his surprise, though, Simon's friends took absolutely no notice of this woman. It was as if she didn't exist. They continued to chat and goof around as though she wasn't even there.

"That was when the idea really came to me. I had to make people notice."

"Why did you commit the murders in England?" asked Wilkins.

"Well of course I originally planned to commit . . . to make, uh, the statement back in Canada. But then I got this travel grant from the Canada Council. I'd applied for one last fall and forgotten all about it. So my plans were derailed a bit, and I came here to have the exhibit."

"And you decided to stay?"

"Yes," replied Simms. "I like it here. I found a cheap place to live and had enough money left from the grant and my student loan to keep me going for a while."

Simms paused. "It's amazing how people let down their guard when they're travelling," he said, echoing Hay's thoughts from earlier in the investigation. "It was surprisingly easy to find girls to talk to. That was the really easy part."

"Where did you get the Rohypnol?" asked Wilkins suddenly.

Simms shrugged. "It's easy to find. Just a pub. Can show you which one if you like," he added helpfully.

"I had to experiment a bit with the dose on Sophie—I think I gave her too much at first and she almost didn't make it to the right spot before I smothered her."

"With your airline cushion."

Simms agreed with that observation.

"After that I tried to be more careful. I kept my eyes open, and then I met Susan Beck. I was a bit concerned that she was also staying at the Wilkommen, but it didn't seem like a big deal and nobody paid me any attention. Just another guy around a place full of guys just like me."

Not just like you, sunshine, thought Hay, mentally vowing to give a rollicking to the police who had been on the scene at the hostel and not noticed this guy occasionally coming and going.

"After that, of course, I decided to try somewhere else, and that's when I met Jenny. Clever girl, that Jenny," said Simms, admiringly. "Interesting to talk to. But I don't know what happened. The Rohypnol didn't seem to work. She was no bigger than Sophie or Susan, so I don't know what happened."

Hay decided not to tell him at that moment that Jenny had ditched one of her drinks, thereby saving her own life.

Simms went on, "I tried out a British accent on her. She

seemed to like it." He glanced at Wilkins and explained, "I minored in drama." Wilkins looked down at his notepad, raising his eyebrows in disbelief.

"Did you smother them when they were on their backs?" asked Hay abruptly, genuinely curious.

"Of course. Too hard to do a good job of it any other way."

"Then," continued Wilkins, looking doubtfully at the stringy man in front of him, "how did you get the girls on their sides?"

"Easier than you would think. You just roll each body part separately. Soon the whole body is on its side. Then I could make her look even prettier, drape the hair, arrange the legs." He stared wistfully at the wall.

"What did you do with their clothes and stuff?" asked Wilkins.

"Stuffed them in my back-pack and threw them in the river. Easily done. Just off the back of Battersea Park. Loads of quiet places along the river, if you pick your times right." He shrugged at this smallest of details.

"Weren't you afraid you'd get caught?" asked Wilkins.

Simms looked up, surprised. "Of course I'd get caught. I was going to continue until I did. I mean, I wasn't going out of my way to get caught or anything." He sat a bit taller in his chair. "I was pretty damned careful about the planning. Had the places picked out early on and made sure there were no CCTV cameras around or anything obvious like that. I didn't think you'd get me quite this quickly, though," he said in grudging admiration. "I thought I'd manage at least five."

There was a long pause. Finally Hay asked softly, "and

the marks. The marks on the girls." This was important. The existence of the marks left by the killer on the hips of the dead girls hadn't been made known to the press. It wouldn't be the first time a suspect decided to plead not guilty after confessing, despite the tape recorder quietly whirring from its ledge on the wall. If Simms acknowledged the marks, they had him, without doubt.

"What about them?" asked Simms.

Hay exhaled deeply. "Those were signatures, weren't they?"

"Yes."

"But the word didn't begin with an *S*, for Simms. What was it?"

"It was Falk, of course," said Simms, astonished.

Hay and Wilkins looked at him blankly.

"Ozvald Falk?" Simms stared in amazement. "Seventeenth-century Norwegian painter? Specializing in beautiful nudes of large women?"

Hay shook his head slightly and Wilkins shrugged his shoulders.

Simms slumped back in his chair, gazing in astonishment at these philistines.

"Okay then," continued Hay. "So Jenny tells us you called yourself Drew. Drew something or other."

"It was meant to be Willis. Drew Willis." He paused, then looked again at the police.

"Get it? I'm supposed to be an artist, right? Drew?"

TWENTY-SEVEN

"How did Mme Bouchard take it?" asked Wilkins over a long-overdue beer later that afternoon, having left Simms in custody, awaiting a long-overdue psychiatric assessment.

Hay and Wilkins were seated in a booth at Hay's favourite pub, the Bull's Head. Wilkins always felt rather privileged when invited to Hay's own local. The landlord brought them their pints, then resumed his usual position behind the bar, today holding court with three of his regular punters.

Hay had called Mme Marie Bouchard, mother of the first victim, Sophie, in Montreal as soon as possible following the arrest of Simms. Hay frowned, shook his head, and tasted his pint.

"Of course she was very happy that we have him in custody and that he won't be able to do this to anyone else" he said. "And she was pleased that I'd phoned to tell her that we got the bastard. But she sounds, what, broken I suppose. I don't expect she'll ever get over it. Not completely, anyway, poor woman."

"What did you make of Simms?" asked Wilkins.

"I honestly don't know what to think," Hay answered, swirling his drink slowly. "Of course he's a nutter and he's dangerous. No question there. But I figure in his own twisted way what he was doing made sense."

Hay shook his head quickly as though to get some unwanted images out of his head, then said, "Anyhow, how did you get on with your psychic?"

"Well, it was interesting," said Wilkins, putting his glass down on the coaster before him. "She said she kept seeing newspapers with brightly coloured pictures in them. That has to do with art, doesn't it, Sir?"

"Perhaps."

"And she thought he wasn't from here."

"Well of course the papers said the victims had been staying in hostels. Not a great leap."

"Well, I think she was pretty good," said Wilkins. "She also, well, like last time . . . ," he trailed off, took a gulp of beer, and stared down at the rings on the table left by numerous past customers.

"Like last time?"

"Said something about somebody with a name like Amber or Ruby, or something like that, wasn't good for me."

Hay raised his eyebrows and studied Wilkins. "Something like Gemma?"

Wilkins didn't meet his boss's eyes. He hadn't told Hay that he and Gemma were finished and didn't feel much like talking about it. For his part, Hay decided to steer clear of the quagmire that was Richard Wilkins's relationship with the stunning and needy Gemma, and quickly changed the subject.

"So what do you think of our Inspector de Jong?" asked Hay.

"Good enough bloke, I guess. Seemed to get stuck in like everyone else. Handsome bugger." Wilkins took another swig of beer and thought for a moment, then added, "Probably more Gemma's type."

Hay looked quickly at his sergeant, who now sat moodily staring into his glass. There not being much of an answer to that, Hay leaned back in his chair, emptied his glass, and reminded Wilkins it was his round.

TWENTY-EIGHT

The following Friday evening, Hay drove to Bramshill to collect Liz. They had planned a dinner at one of the local inns, which he'd heard good reports about. Freed of the burden of solving the mystery of the murdered young women, he felt especially light-hearted as he drove his old Rover to the police college.

He pulled into the circular drive in front of the impressive mansion and stopped by the front entrance after presenting his warrant card to a police guard. A handsome blond man was hanging about the entrance and attempted to engage Liz in conversation as she exited the front doors.

Hay allowed himself a moment of adolescent smugness as Liz gave the man a friendly hello without actually looking at him, waved at Hay, and approached the Rover. As he walked around to open the car door, he glanced at the young man, who looked at him sullenly and re-entered the college. Hay supposed, correctly, that this was Liz's Australian colleague.

Liz was happy to be back in Hay's old Rover, in which she had ridden on several occasions during their joint investigation of the Guévin murder at the High Commission in London. It seemed an age ago. But the car was the same, slightly beat up but clean, apart from the ashtray. Hay had clearly made an effort, as he had emptied it prior to leaving to collect Liz, but a couple of butts had recently been deposited there, and the small compartment was lined with white ash.

He had arrived at six o'clock precisely—early for a dinner date, but they looked forward to a lot of time together with a few quiet drinks in the pub before dinner. They drove along a narrow road past fields, farmhouses, and low stone walls as the evening closed in. Rain began to spatter the windshield in short bursts.

After some small talk and a couple of cigarettes, they saw a sign announcing that they were entering the village of Eversley. Hay found the country inn quite easily, although it was his first visit there. A converted farmhouse of red brick almost obscured by thriving ivy, the Grey Horse presented a cozy spot for a quiet dinner.

"I picked it in part because of the name," said Hay with a smile, "but the food's meant to be good." They dashed from the parking lot to the double doors, huddled under Hay's large umbrella. It had begun to rain quite steadily now.

Liz wouldn't have cared if the food was inedible: she loved the cozy pub with its roaring wood fire and ancient bar. It was quiet. There weren't too many patrons this evening, or perhaps they would come in later. They chose a comfortable-looking table near the fireplace and ordered a bottle of Bordeaux.

In answer to Liz's myriad questions, Hay was detailing the circumstances surrounding the apprehension of Simon Simms, although he seemed slightly uncomfortable as he related the events.

She shook her head. "Another Canadian," she said.

Hay was tasting the wine, of which he approved, and the portly waiter poured them both a glass and handed them menus. He assessed, correctly, that they would take a while to place their orders and went back to polishing his bar.

"Yes," agreed Hay, "My sister-in-law, Helena, once remarked that you Canadians 'seem to get into quite a lot of trouble over here.'" He laughed, a bit dryly.

"I suppose we do," she agreed, smiling. He didn't respond to her smile, looking straight over her shoulder instead. "What about that reporter?" asked Liz conversationally. "He was looking good for a while, yes?"

Liz noticed again that Hay seemed a bit uncomfortable, not his usual composed self. She rapidly went through things she might have said or done to annoy him but came up blank.

"Lombardy," Hay acknowledged. "Just a punk freelance reporter from Essex trying to make a name for himself. Occasionally claimed to be attached to one newspaper or another, but he wasn't on anybody's staff. We never even came up with anything with his byline on it."

Hay knocked back some wine, as though very thirsty, not at all in keeping with his usual respectful approach to the beverage. "Must say, though," he said, swallowing, "he was pretty thorough and did his damnedest to get a break on the story. He may eventually do well."

Liz nodded and pulled a cigarette from her purse, at the same time sneaking a look in her purse mirror to see if she had lipstick on her teeth or a pimple had erupted on her nose, but she didn't notice anything glaringly obvious. She lit her cigarette, knowing it was bad form to smoke and drink good wine at the same time, as the smoke would distort the taste. But clearly both of them had the same bad habit, as Hay then lit one of his own. She noticed he had not offered her a light.

She was feeling a little uneasy, as their usual easy camaraderie was plainly lacking this evening. "I think I'm, er, getting a bit hungry," said Liz, picking up her menu. Hay nodded absently and looked, unsmiling, at his own. Eventually he chose shepherd's pie and she ordered scotch eggs.

"I've always wanted to try those," she said, with a cheerful smile.

"Don't like 'em myself," he said gruffly. "Greasy."

Liz took an unladylike slug of her wine this time. She was beginning to get annoyed. He was a moody bugger. He'd hardly even made eye contact with her since they'd been in the restaurant. This wasn't at all what she had expected. *Unless he's decided that pursuing this any further would be impossible*, she thought, acknowledging that, in her more objective moments, she had frequently reached the same conclusion. *He's probably right*, she thought, and studied some colourful hunting prints on the wall opposite her. *Or maybe he's just gone off me.*

She glanced back at Hay. By this point he look decidedly odd. Perhaps she had misjudged his manner? Maybe he was actually ill?

Abruptly, as though he wanted to get it over with—which, in fact, he did—Hay said, "Look Liz. I don't know what the hell is going to happen with us. But I have to confess I'm utterly smitten with you and I don't know what to do about it."

Liz exhaled with relief, feeling almost as though she wanted to slump from her chair onto the floor, but instead she quickly confessed that her sentiments matched his. Although, like him, she didn't know what they should do about it.

Their meals came, although later Liz couldn't remember if she liked scotch eggs or not. Afterward, they smoked in silence, slowly finishing their bottle of wine. The fire crackled and spat, and an occasional clang emanated from the kitchen, but it was otherwise a quiet evening at the Grey Horse.

"Okay," she said. "We clearly have a lot to think about. So why don't we just enjoy our evening and the fact that

I'm here for another week. We can think about everything tomorrow."

"You mean," he said, remembering the movie, "something like 'we'll think about it at Tara'?"

Liz smiled at the reference. She loved old movies too. "Something very like that, yes."

ACKNOWLEDGEMENTS

I must express once again my gratitude to Taryn Boyd and her team at TouchWood Editions for their diligence and professionalism in the production and publication of *Measured for Murder*. As always, many thanks to my editor, Frances Thorsen, for combining a comprehensive vision for the book with a sharp eye for detail.

I cannot sufficiently thank the experts on whom I've depended not only for this book but for my previous Forsyth and Hay novels as well. The insight and professional expertise of this small, accomplished group have made me comfortable and confident in the detail in the books, and I'm delighted that this professional input has led to close friendships. So thanks very much to RCMP Chief Superintendent Lynn Twardosky (ret'd); RCMP Superintendent MSM Claude Theriault (ret'd); BC coroner Barbara McLintock; and Eric Hussey (ret'd) of the Metropolitan Police, London.

Many thanks are also due to Sidney businesses Pharmasave and Tanner's Books for their support and for the opportunities they have provided to assist in the promotion of the Forsyth and Hay series—not to mention the personal "atta-girls," which are always more than welcome during the writing and production of a book.

My brother Cliff Wilkinson and his wife Julie and her family, and my sister-in-law Chantal, have been consistently rock-solid in their support of my literary ventures, for which I am continually and sincerely grateful. I also offer my heartfelt thanks to my dear, long-time friends Alison Green; Ann Cronin-Cossette; Christine Rollo; Lee Emerson; and the Meat Draw Girls for their support and encouragement. For the solid and enthusiastic support of newer friends Ray Billard, Ken Brind, and Chad Ganske, thank so much, guys. Much appreciated!

Finally, I am very grateful to all my friends and supporters, for whom there is inadequate room here to mention individually. Thanks so much for accompanying me during this extraordinary process.

Before taking to crime writing, JANET BRONS worked as a foreign affairs consultant following a seventeen-year career in the Canadian foreign service, with postings in Kuala Lumpur, Warsaw, and Moscow. She holds a master of arts in political science and international relations. *Measured for Murder* is the third installment in her Forsyth and Hay mystery series. Brons lives in Sidney, British Columbia.